Quentin looked like sex

Living breathing sex. From the glint in his eyes that reminded Shandi of what they'd done last night, to the way his hair appeared to have been styled by a lover while she writhed beneath him.

Living breathing sex... As much as Shandi tried to focus on something else, she finally had to back away and sit down. And try not to drool.

Okay, it wasn't that bad. She tried her best to remain analytical, almost critical. Like a spectator watching a show.

Nothing. It wasn't working. All she could think about was getting her hands on Quentin, kissing him, tearing off his clothes. That and the way he made her laugh and hope, the way he teased her...

He was a good man and he cared about her future, her happiness. About her.

And seeing him now, straddling the bar chair in reverse, his arms braced along the top, his feet hooked on the rungs, the fit of his clothes revealing the body beneath...

Oh, but she was in such serious trouble here.

Blaze™

Dear Reader,

One of the things I most love about writing for Harlequin Blaze
is the chance to work on miniseries with other authors. I first
did it with Jo Leigh and Isabel Sharpe on MEN TO DO. This
time, for DO NOT DISTURB, we've shared the good fun with
Nancy Warren, Debbi Rawlins and Jill Shalvis. It's amazing what
can happen when the pot of imagination is stirred by so many
creative minds.

Kiss & Makeup, my contribution profiling the erotic boutique hotel
Hush, tells the story of bartender Shandi Fossey, who's come to
New York for a career as a makeup artist. She's excited, optimistic
and she runs smack-dab into the cynical Quentin Marks.

Yes, *that* Quentin Marks. The same one you met in my 1999
fifteenth anniversary Harlequin Temptation, *Four Men & a Lady.*
Quentin is older, wiser and much more pessimistic than any man
should be. And he's ready to go home to Austin, to leave the
limelight of his Grammy-winning career behind. Except now that
means leaving Shandi, as well.

I hope you enjoy their story, and that you'll visit all of us at
www.hush-hotel.com for an inside peek at Hush. And don't forget
to check out my special linked online story at eHarlequin.com.
Finally, look for the next DO NOT DISTURB story,
Private Relations by Nancy Warren, available in October.

Best,

Alison Kent

KISS & MAKEUP
Alison Kent

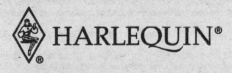

HARLEQUIN®

TORONTO • NEW YORK • LONDON
AMSTERDAM • PARIS • SYDNEY • HAMBURG
STOCKHOLM • ATHENS • TOKYO • MILAN • MADRID
PRAGUE • WARSAW • BUDAPEST • AUCKLAND

With great fondness and respect to the hardworking, hard brainstorming, hard-to-beat friends who made this project so much fun: Jo Leigh, Isabel Sharpe, Nancy Warren, Debbi Rawlins and Jill Shalvis. Uh, let's not do it again any time soon! Also to Birgit Davis-Todd for helping to pull the project together. I'll call Hush and make reservations for seven, k?

ISBN 0-373-79201-8

KISS & MAKEUP

www.eHarlequin.com

Printed in U.S.A.

1

To Shandi Fossey, the sky was the limit. And if there was one thing she missed about Round-Up, Oklahoma, that was it. The sky. Pinpoints of white light twinkling in an inky black bowl. Cotton-ball clouds scooped high on a pale blue plate. Butter spreading at dawn. Orange Julius at sunset.

The sky above Manhattan was about wedges cut between buildings, streetlights reflected in windowpanes and flashing neon colors—or so it seemed, sitting as she was, cross-legged and lights-off in front of the floor-to-ceiling windows of her sixth-floor West Village apartment at three-thirty in the morning.

But that was okay. The wedges thing. Really. Because there were lights a whole lot brighter and much more meaningful here in the Big Apple than found anywhere in the sky over Oklahoma.

And that was why she was here, wasn't it? For the lights on Broadway as well as those off. The theaters and cabarets, sets and stages and clubs. All of those myriad places offering canvases for her work.

Eyelids and lashes and lips. Brows and cheekbones.

The slope of a nose. The line of a jaw. These were the landscapes she transformed, shaping and coloring and creating, turning the ordinary into the fantastic with her brushes and sponges, her pots and tubes and jars of colors and creams.

She leaned her upper body to the left, stretching dozens of muscles as she draped her right arm as far as she could over her head and down toward the floor. Her shift as bartender at Erotique in the hotel Hush meant long hours on her feet at least five nights a week, many times six.

Afterward, unwinding beneath her own personal wedge of what sky she could see had become her routine. She enjoyed the silence, the dark, the sense of so much life teeming around her—even though what life she could see from here was so very, very still.

She imagined patrons talking long into the night, discussing and arguing over the shows they'd seen. She pictured the ushers, hostesses and attendants waiting for the venues to empty so they could kick off their shoes, along with their frozen smiles.

She thought of the actors easing out of their roles much as she eased from hers when she sat here each night, leaving behind the Shandi who mixed martinis and margaritas for Erotique's sophisticated clientele and slipping—reluctantly? regretfully? naturally?—back into the role she'd lived so long.

That of a long-legged, willowy cat's tail of a filly from Oklahoma—the description she'd been tagged with by the beer-and-whiskey crowd at the Thirsty Rattler, her family's bar in the small town of Round-Up.

One of these days she would figure out which of the two women she was, whether she needed to make a choice between them or combine them. Had she left Oklahoma to encouraging farewells instead of predictions that she'd return in six months, her tail tucked between her legs, she might find that integration a whole lot easier.

As it was, there was a big part of her that just couldn't let go of the doubts planted by her family when she'd announced her decision to leave Round-Up for a life in New York City.

For the last year she'd been pursuing a bachelor of science degree in cosmetics and fragrance marketing at the Fashion Institute of Technology. During that time she temped for a living—most recently at the law firm of Winslow, Reynolds and Forster—until hearing whispers around the office about the opening of Hush.

And for the same very long year she'd been satisfied with the status quo of her studies, her work schedule and her friends, needing nothing more. Or so she had thought.

Until tonight, when *he* had sat down at the bar.

She realigned her body to stretch her left side, her fingertips hovering over the hardwood floor at her right hip. Oh, but if he hadn't been the most gorgeous thing she'd ever seen. Better even than the actor from that television show about Navy investigators, who had stayed at Hush during the hotel's grand opening.

Only this guy was real, not an elusive Hollywood fantasy. One who'd wanted to talk to her. Thankfully Erotique had been busy beyond belief, giving her a legitimate excuse to walk away and catch her breath when their flirtation took on a sexually dangerous edge, as it had so quickly.

At least walking away had worked tonight.

But he was a guest at Hush, meaning the odds were that she would be seeing him again. And the bar wouldn't always be as hopping as it had been this evening. He was going to lose interest if she couldn't get her act together and keep her mind—and her ever-wavering sense of self-worth—out of Round-Up.

Keeping her mind out of the bedroom was an entirely separate matter. It was hard to talk to the man when she couldn't stop herself from thinking about getting him out of his clothes, but that's exactly how she'd spent a large chunk of the night's long shift.

His hair was blond, or had been when he was younger. It had darkened, leaving him with lo-lights instead of high. And it was long, a bit wavy—a leonine mane. He wore it pulled back and wore a goatee and soul patch, as well.

His smile twinkled. His eyes twinkled. His personality, too. She'd had the best time exchanging bantering quips and innuendo. She'd appreciated his wit. Appreciated, too, calls from the other patrons allowing her to step away and gather her thoughts while mixing drinks and serving.

She'd asked him what had brought him to the city and to the hotel. He'd told her it was a business trip— the business of money, music and women. She'd teased back that she wasn't much for helping him with the first two, but the third....

For a long moment then he'd held her gaze, and she'd imagined his fingers that were slowly stroking his glass stroking her instead. Her body had responded, her filmy bra beneath her sleeveless black tuxedo shirt doing little good to keep her private thoughts private. He'd noticed. He'd lifted his drink, his eyes on her as he'd swallowed, his throat working, his jaw taut, the vein at his temple pulsing.

Blood had pulsed through her body, too. It did the same now as she remembered the way he'd looked at her. As if he wanted to strip her bare, to eat her up, to discover how well their bodies fit together, to devour her once he had.

And then she wondered if he truly understood where it was he was staying. How perfect a setting Hush made for a steamy affair.

She smiled as she thought of the words the media had used to describe the hotel when it had initially opened. The brainchild of heiress Piper Devon, Hush had been called *the* place for *the young, the rich and the horny.* Shandi, of course, knew it was much more than that— no matter the truth to the adage that sex sells. The business of Hush wasn't as much sex, however, as it was sensuality.

Rich perfumes were found in each room's candles,

bath salts, shower gels and massage oils. Private video cameras, video collections and boxes of stimulating toys encouraged tactile intimacy. Whether enjoying a midnight swim by moonlight in the rooftop pool or the basement sofa bar's music and erotic performance art, guests were guaranteed privacy, discretion and the freedom to explore.

Then there was the pure visually artistic appeal of the place. The hotel's vintage and original artwork made for the perfect complement to the 1920s art-deco theme done in black, pink, gray and sea-foam green. What Hush was could only be described as a luxurious feast for the senses.

And at that, Shandi's thoughts returned to the man she'd met tonight at the bar. *Yeah,* she mused, sighing deeply as she stretched out both legs in front of her, leaning forward to grab her toes. Another very long shift lay ahead. And she was already anxious to get back to work, to see him again. And for a simple reason, really.

He was the first man since her arrival in New York to have her thinking beyond work and school to the physical things that occurred between a man and a woman. Those things she wanted. Those things she missed. Those things she hadn't taken time to pursue since moving here and settling in and scheduling every hour of every day of her way-too-busy life.

When she heard a key in the front door behind her, she screwed up her mouth and shook her head. Speaking of busy, at least she didn't have class tomorrow until noon. Evan Harcourt, her roommate, who was in FIT's master's program in illustration, having switched gears after years spent in photography, had to be on campus at eight.

Silly man, keeping the working and dating schedule he did, even now at the beginning of September's new term. She waited until he'd closed and locked the door before speaking.

"The things men do for love."

Evan jumped, cursed swiftly and under his breath. "I swear, Shandi, if I end up dead from a heart attack, I'm going to kick your ass."

She listened to his steps as he crossed the room. "That'll be hard to do from the grave. Unless you come back as Angel or Spike."

"Smart-ass," he mumbled, dropping to his haunches behind her and massaging her shoulders, as was his routine when finding her here after work. "I'll get April to do it for me then. Vengeance and all that."

"Hmm," Shandi murmured, halfway pondering Evan's shaky romance, halfway out of her mind with a pleasure that was purely platonic.

April Carter, Evan's girlfriend for a year now who was majoring at FIT in jewelry design, had definitely lucked out, snagging a man with amazingly talented hands.

And that thought had Shandi's mind returning again to Erotique and picturing the way *he* had used *his* hands tonight, holding his glass, stroking the crystal tumbler the way she'd wanted him to hold and stroke her.

With a sigh she returned to the moment. "What

makes you think April would lift a finger on your say-so? Your dead say-so at that? You can't even get her to introduce you to her parents."

At her prodding of a sore spot that was none of her business, Evan backed off and away. "What's that? Your shoulders aren't aching tonight as usual?"

Grr. "That dead ass-kicking you're threatening me with? You're about to see the real-life version if you don't bring those hands back over here now."

"Oh, well, when you ask so nicely…" The sentence trailed, but he did scoot in behind her and resume the massage for which a licensed masseuse would charge a night's worth of Shandi's tips, if not more.

She supposed she really shouldn't rag on Evan about his romance with April. On the one hand, the couple had everything going for them—and had ever since the night a year ago when they'd met at the Starbucks where Evan still worked, though he'd since moved up into management.

Shared interests, similar goals, amazingly compatible personalities. An attraction undeniable by anyone who spent time in the same room with the two—even if they stood on opposite sides.

On the other hand, April's family weighed down the scales until even Shandi doubted that Evan and April's romance could weather the storm brought on by the Carters' expectations as to what made an appropriate marriage match.

Sometimes love just wasn't enough—a truth that

strangely brought her thoughts back to *him* one more time. And for the first time to a subject other than sex.

He was obviously high powered enough, wealthy enough, well enough connected to be staying at Hush. And that meant what? He'd take one look at Shandi Fossey from Round-Up, Oklahoma—only one, in his rearview mirror—and that would be that? The end of her own fantasy fling?

And why was she even going there? What did it matter what he thought? Especially when she wasn't looking to do anything more than get him out of his designer duds and into her bed.

You can take the girl out of Oklahoma, Shandi, but Oklahoma stays forever in the girl.

"Yes, Daddy," she grumbled under her breath. "I hear you loud and clear."

"Talking to yourself again?" Evan asked.

Her head bobbed with the motion of his hands when he kneaded the base of her skull. "Thinking about you and April."

"Funny. I could've sworn you were calling me Daddy."

She couldn't help but grin. "If I were going to call anyone Daddy, it would be this guy tonight who spent most of my shift sitting at the bar."

"Hmm. A sugar daddy with one foot on a banana peel and one foot in the grave?"

Shandi swung around and swatted Evan's shoulder. "Hey, that's *so* not funny."

He shifted to face her, one wrist draped over one

raised knee as he sat. "No, but you and I are in the same broke-as-a-beggar boat." He grinned, his smile bright in the room's low light. "Why do you think I'm dating April?"

"If you say for her money, I'm going to hit you again, buddy." Shandi did her best schoolteacher finger shake. "Besides, you're not exactly a pauper."

"My grandmother's not a pauper, you mean. I'm poorer than dirt."

And Shandi knew that really he was. That his grandmother let him—and by association let her—live rent-free in this, one of several apartments she owned in the city. As long as he paid his own way through school.

And as long as he didn't live with April in sin.

No grandson of Ellen Harcourt's was going to take up with a girl who'd never had to work for a thing in her life.

"Do you think it matters?" Shandi asked him. "Being attracted to someone totally out of your league?"

"Are you talking about me and April? Or you and banana man?" When she glared, he went on. "Being attracted, no. Who can help it?"

"Those of us not thinking with a penis?"

"That's bull, Shandi. A woman's just as likely to make a move because she wants in a guy's pants as a guy is. Uh, as a guy is who wants in a woman's pants. Whatever. You know what I mean."

Shandi chuckled. Then sobered, thinking more about her mystery man's eyes, more about his hungry, burning look, the devastating way she'd found herself wanting to help him get her naked.

Dear Lord, she was losing her mind. "Is that a bad thing? Wanting in a guy's pants?"

Evan blew out a breath heavy with his reluctance to talk. Had she been prying about baseball, he'd be animated and all up in her face yammering on about the Yankees.

Instead he pulled up his other knee and rolled down to lie on his back, feet flat on the floor, his head pillowed on his wrists, his dark hair sweeping the cherry wood planks.

"I'm waiting over here," she finally said, once again sitting cross-legged.

"It's still a double standard, Shandi—the women a guy takes to bed and the one he takes home."

That particular truth really sucked, yet in this case it was more the reverse of the situation that she couldn't let go. She shouldn't be so hung up, but with Evan and April both her very best friends, it was hard to think of either hurting the other. Or either getting hurt.

Her concern was strictly that of a friend in the middle. A sucky place to be. "So why doesn't April take you home? She doesn't want her parents to know she has a lover?"

He waited a long time before answering, clearing the hesitation from his throat before he did. "April and I aren't lovers. And if you tell her I told you that, the ass-kicking switches into high gear."

What? Speechless. She was absolutely speechless, her mouth as dry as a bone. April hadn't once hinted that she wasn't sleeping with Evan. She'd hinted at quite the opposite, in fact.

"I don't get it. You've spent the night over there—"

"On the couch."

Unbelievable. "Not in her bed?"

"Nope."

"Never?"

"Never."

"Huh." Shandi didn't even know what to say. "Has she said why? I mean, I'm assuming you've tried or told her you want to." And then a pause as she thought. "You do want to, right? Or is this more of that double-standard thing?"

"Do we have to talk about this? I've got class in four hours."

"Drawing? Skip it." He wouldn't, and she ought to let him off the hook, but he was her only window into the male psyche.

The only one whose brain she could pick about what to do with her crush on tonight's customer. "I need to know what men think."

"Why?" He turned his head sharply. "Are you planning to hit on banana man?"

She shoved at his closest knee, rocking both of his legs. "Would you stop calling him that?"

"What's his name?"

"Quentin."

"And you want to sleep with him."

"I don't know." She did, of course, hating how these ridiculous double standards men embraced labeled her because of that want. "He intrigues me. That's all."

"Right." A snort. "It's not like you want to do him because he's hot."

Okay, yes, there was that. An attitude she'd always shared with April. Or so she'd thought. But if April wasn't even sleeping with Evan, the man she loved...

This complicated love and sex and lust business was for the birds. Shandi wanted things plain and simple, to act on her attraction to Quentin without having him think less of her for doing so.

Because what he thought of her mattered just as much as having him want her. "Okay. I admit it. I'm obviously a hopeless slut."

"Sluts are good."

She groaned with frustration, then lay back beside Evan. "Good when I'm the slut in question. Just not when it's April."

"Shandi, this conversation is putting me to sleep."

She ignored him. "You know I'm going to have to rag on April for not telling me the truth."

"What?" Evan perked up. "She told you we were having sex?"

Good. The reaction she'd wanted. "No, but she let me think so. Heck, you let me think so. I mean, I don't get it, but if her not sleeping with you makes her a better catch—"

"It's not about her being a better catch." He sighed. "It's just that by the time we realized we were more than friends, we were such *good* friends we didn't want to ruin it by sleeping together. Not until we were sure it was more."

"It is more, isn't it?"

"Yeah. It's more." This time his sigh was pure poetry.

And hers pure envy. She wanted that same more. She really, truly wanted that very same more. "So this guy at the hotel. Quentin. I shouldn't sleep with him then."

"Depends."

"On what?"

"On whether you're interested in more than his banana."

QUENTIN MARKS STOOD STARING out the window of his sixteenth-floor suite. He had a meeting at nine. He needed to be in bed. Check that. He needed to be asleep.

Except, being in bed made him think of being there for sex and being there with Shandi Fossey.

He had never met a woman with legs like those of Erotique's bartender. And that was saying a lot considering the legs he'd seen in his lifetime.

A man didn't get to be a Grammy-winning record producer without being subjected to a hell of a lot of exposure—perpetrated by women—and more than a few men—wanting his attention, looking to gain an industry in. Using him. Willing to do anything, give him anything, promise him the sexual moon if he would simply listen to their demo, make an introduction, reveal the secrets to success he was a greedy bastard for keeping to himself.

Yeah. He was a bastard all right. A bastard because he looked out for himself, he mused, stepping from the corner room's window to the balcony overlooking Madison Avenue and pulling open the French doors. The night air was muggy, the lights muted, the noise level low enough that he had no trouble hearing his thoughts.

He wasn't sure if that was good or bad considering lately his thoughts were all about getting back to Austin. And until he took care of business here, made his deals, got what he wanted, he couldn't go back. He couldn't go home.

Home.

He sighed, drained the rest of the brandy that room service had delivered, compliments of management. Quentin had to admit the rumors were true. Hush was *the* place to stay—even if he'd originally planned to stay elsewhere.

It was the hotel's name that had drawn him. It had drawn his assistant's attention, as well; she'd been the one to show him its promotional material. Later she'd shown him the write-up in the *New Yorker* profiling the Devon hotel empire and this newest venture that was run—quite successfully—by the daughter, Piper, whose wild-child reputation was one those in the business knew well.

He'd flipped through both the brochure and the magazine, curious, not as interested in the amenities as much as the privacy said amenities obviously entailed. He wanted his visit to the city to be a quiet one. He wanted to get in, get his business done and get out without a lot of fanfare. He was winding down that part of his life, the one that kept him in the limelight.

He'd reserved the hotel's basement conference center for two separate meetings tomorrow—uh, make that today—as well as more later in the week. In the past he'd never had reason to be as involved with the industry's money men as he was now.

But now he had to be. Now was all about his own studio. The Marks label: Markin' It Up. Finally setting himself up in Austin and going home to stay. Making that dream happen was why he was here. Getting the backing he needed wasn't going to be the problem. Deciding who he wanted behind him was.

Right now, however, the thought forefront in his mind wasn't about financing but about sex. As strange as it sounded, as strange as it felt, his studio plans had kept him too busy these last months to do more than mentally indulge.

Now he wanted more. Now he wanted Shandi. A woman he shouldn't have wanted at all. They hadn't talked much in the way of specifics; no real getting-to-know-you conversation had found its way into their back-and-forth.

But what she *had* told him was enough to have made him want to push back from the bar and do his drinking elsewhere. In a quiet corner. At a dark table. Away from her smile and her big blue eyes. But he hadn't. He'd stayed there with her and drunk her up, too.

She was majoring in cosmetics and marketing, headed for a career—she hoped, the marketing was a fall-back plan— in the theater, in film, in music videos. Wherever she could find work as a makeup artist in the entertainment industry. The marketing was a fall-back plan.

His industry.

An industry that crushed dreams daily.

He'd been lucky to live his. Others weren't so lucky. *Most* weren't so.

She was a clichéd breath of fresh air when he was used to inhaling lungfuls of jaded cynicism.

Hell, these days he didn't even like listening to himself think, what with the way his own thoughts were so polluted. He didn't blame Shandi for not sticking around for more conversation beyond the flirting they'd done. He knew he'd been nowhere near as entertaining as her animated responses had made him out to be.

Then again, he wasn't blind, deaf or dumb to where her attention tended to drift when she'd thought him not looking, when she'd feigned interest in the other bar patrons.

That interest was what was keeping him up, keeping him awake, keeping him from listening to his years of experience and the common sense that came with it.

He was hard-bitten; she was exuberantly optimistic. He was turning his back on the bright lights of the big city she so openly embraced.

He was weary of witnessing the implosion of dreams. She wore hope with the same authority, the same familiar comfort with which she wore her uniform of tuxedo pants and shirt.

And all he could think about was getting her out of the one without damaging the other.

2

Attention: EVERYONE!
The cocktail napkins are NOT to be used
to clean up spills or for handkerchiefs,
makeup cloths or whatever picnics
you have going on in the bar's back room.
BRING YOUR OWN BOUNTY OR BRAWNY!
Armand & Shandi

QUENTIN IMPATIENTLY WAITED for Shandi to begin the evening shift at the bar.

It had been midafternoon before he'd finished the second of his scheduled meetings and accompanied his business advisor and the bank's trio of officers from the basement conference center to the lobby.

The group had lingered long enough sharing financial war stories that Quentin had finally suggested a drink—a multipurpose suggestion. He'd felt like a fool paying more attention to the comings and goings in the bar than to the conversation.

At least *in* the bar his distraction wouldn't be as obvious, his obsession as apparent. By the time the others had left an hour later, however, Shandi still hadn't put in an appearance. Quentin then decided on an early and solitary dinner.

He'd convinced the hostess in the hotel restaurant, Amuse Bouche, to seat him where he had a clear view of Erotique. He finally caught sight of Shandi, of course, the minute his server walked away after placing his salad of seared Norwegian salmon, mixed greens, cucumbers and yellow-pepper vinaigrette on the table.

His first instinct was to rush through his meal and hurry into the bar. But then he realized how very much he enjoyed simply looking at her, watching her and doing it while she remained unaware. He usually didn't have the benefit of flying under the radar and he took full advantage.

She looked completely at ease, dodging the other bartender, weaving in and out and around as they both filled orders, mixed drinks, poured, served and chatted up patrons. She smiled and laughed, her face expressive and engaged, fresh. She enjoyed herself as she worked. It showed. He liked it. And he found himself relaxing while he ate.

He took his time and let his anticipation build. He tasted little of the food on his plate and didn't touch the complimentary wine a female diner sent over. It wasn't food or drink his appetite required. And he didn't want to feel obligated because of the gift and get caught up by a conversation in which he had zero interest.

His only interest was Shandi. Thing was, he wanted more from her than sex. He wanted to see her smile for him, at him, because of him. He wanted to share her optimism, her outlook, her disposition. And then he wanted it all so suddenly that the distance between them was too much, the wait unnecessary.

He signaled for his server, paid for his meal and headed for Erotique.

"How did your meetings go?" Shandi asked as he hoisted himself up onto one of the funky black chairs at the half-moon-shaped bar and leaned against the inverted-triangle back.

The lights above, a strangely cool pink shining down from nested fixtures, turned her blond hair nearly white. Until she cocked her head. And then all he could think about was cotton candy.

He wrapped his hand around the highball glass she set in front of him, focusing on the drink she was pouring instead of her sweetness and the way he wanted her. "Well enough, I suppose. As meetings go."

She laughed lightly, a soft lyrical sound of crystal and bells. "Doesn't sound like meetings are much your thing."

He shrugged. "Depends on the topic."

"And this one was?" she asked, nodding toward another customer who signaled for a drink.

"Money," Quentin said, ice clinking on glass. She gazed at him quizzically before stepping away to deliver the bourbon-and-rocks.

He studied her as she moved, as she talked, taking care of her customer, appearing to give the man her full attention yet all the while aware of the needs of the other bar patrons.

He wondered how long she'd been serving drinks, if it was experience tending bar or her natural ease with people that made her efforts seem effortless.

Then he wondered why Hush had her wearing pants when the business of the hotel was eroticism and the length of her legs defined the word.

He could not get enough of the way she walked, of the sway of her hips, the curves of her ass in motion. He'd settled into this particular seat two nights in a row now for that very reason.

From here he had a clear view of the length of the bar and beyond. And watching her was quickly becoming his favorite pastime.

When she returned to where he was sitting, she picked up their conversation right where she'd left it, asking, "You don't like money?"

"If it's mine, sure. If it's not…" He left the sentence hanging and shrugged. "I don't like being obligated." He also didn't like talking business when he wanted to get to know her.

"Ah, you don't like being in debt, you mean."

This time he shook his head and laughed as much to himself as for her. "A necessary evil, unfortunately."

"Tell me about it." She waved over his head at a cute Gwyneth Paltrow look-alike walking through the lobby. Her eyes danced as she smiled. When he asked, she answered, "That's Kit."

"A friend?"

"She's the director of public relations. We're forever comparing our student loans that rival the national debt.

And I'll probably be paying mine off with my retirement fund since I waited so late to get up the guts to start school."

Hmm. "Why did you need guts to start school?"

"If you want *that* story, you'll be here all night," she replied, a teasing lilt to her voice, a suggestion—one that seemed to be an invitation he do just that. That he insist she tell him. That he stay with her all night.

He wanted to. He just didn't want to do it here. Not with an audience. Not when his room upstairs put a sheikh's palace to shame. So he simply lifted a brow and tapped his fingers on the side of his glass.

Shandi rolled her eyes, her grin charming him, her reluctance intriguing him, her coy flutter of lashes too cute to be anything but real. "You're going to stick around until I tell all, aren't you?"

"I don't have a single place to go or another person to see." She might be teasing him, but the reservation in her voice convinced him not to press any button that would send her skittering away. "I'd say you're stuck with me."

She shook her head slowly, leaned into the corner. Leaned close to him. Still not quite comfortable, but near enough that he knew she wanted to stay.

One dark blond brow arched upward. "Okay, but consider yourself warned. Because when you fall out of your chair from boredom and need stitches on the back of your head, I won't be held responsible."

"Got it," he said and fought back a grin.

She took a deep breath. "It wasn't so much starting school that required the guts as it was moving here against my family's wishes to go. I already had an associate's degree, which I wasn't using, by the way—"

"Why not?"

She stared at the bar's surface, rubbed away a water spot instead of looking at him when she spoke. "Because my parents claimed to need my help at work." She shrugged, gestured with one hand. "They own a bar. Though compared to Erotique, the Rattler's really more of a saloon."

"The Rattler?"

"The Thirsty Rattler." Her grin returned, though almost reluctantly, a shy self-deprecation. "Yeah. If you can believe it."

He believed it and he pictured it and had no problem doing either. "Your accent's not quite Texas…."

"Oklahoma," she provided. "Round-Up, Oklahoma."

"We're almost neighbors then. Except Oklahoma's still a long day's drive from Austin."

"And I don't live in Oklahoma anymore."

He nodded his touché, wondering what about Oklahoma had driven her away, because he was certain that's what had happened. "So your parents wanted you to stay and work. You wanted to leave and study. Either way, someone was going to end up being unhappy."

"That about covers it." She curled her fingers into her palm and considered her nails. "Though I'm not sure *unhappy* is the word I would use."

He sat back in his chair, crossed his hands behind his head. "What word would you use?"

She laughed then. "Depends on who I'm describing."

"Then describe yourself." He was interested in Shandi, not her family. Especially considering her reluctance to talk about herself.

That trait made him all the more curious; most women wanted to tell him every detail of their lives, more than he cared or wanted to know.

He prodded her to go on. "If you'd stayed in Oklahoma, you'd be…what? Bitter? Resentful?"

Nodding, she smoothed a hand back over the hair she wore in a long French braid. "And guilty for feeling either one."

"Because they're your family."

She smiled, the lift of her lips seeming to be more for her own benefit than his. "They may not have my best interests at heart, but I gotta love them anyway. They are who they are, ya know?"

Then she continued, the rush of words making him wonder how long she'd been holding in what came out as frustration. "And it's not even about *my* interests. They don't think that way. The family has always been one entity. The Fosseys. We're not individuals. No one is expected to think outside that communal box. The fact that I did…"

She didn't pick up the trailing sentence right away, so Quentin leaned forward again, one forearm on the sleek ebony bar as if he could close the distance between them. He hated having this conversation here.

The room was growing crowded; he wasn't going to have her to himself much longer. He was enjoying her too much to forgive the interruptions, yet the ugly head of his impatience hardly thrilled him.

What he wanted was to take her downstairs into the basement, where the partitioned banquettes in Exhibit A—the underground bar set up for erotic performance art—offered the privacy Erotique did not.

Except, it would be a privacy swathed in blue lights and smoky darkness and an aura of intimacy more conducive to sex than to talk. He wasn't quite sure either of them was ready to go there.

Sure, sex with Shandi would rock his world. It was her world he worried about. Her world that upped the ante. That made the wait worthwhile.

He cleared his throat and returned to the conversation just as she tossed back her head and glanced up toward the ceiling. "Wow, I have no idea where that came from. It's the customer who's supposed to pour out his heartache. And the bartender who's supposed to offer the shoulder or the ear."

"Are you always this hard on yourself?" he asked softly, because he wondered why she was. Why she didn't want to let go. Didn't want to talk about herself.

"Only most of the time." She shrugged, then brushed some loose hair back from her forehead. "Fallout from my overachiever syndrome."

"Something that runs in the family?"

She stepped away from the bar and laughed. "You are just not giving up, are you?"

"I never do. Not when there's something I want."

She stood there for a moment staring at him, her pulse quickening at the base of her throat. When she smiled, when she tilted her head to the side and grinned, he swore he felt the glass he was holding threaten to crack in his hand.

"Quentin," she started, then paused. "Are you coming on to me?"

He couldn't help the way his mouth crooked up on one side. "I'm doing my best."

"Okay then." She nodded. "I just wanted to make sure."

"And now that you have?"

"I don't know." She gestured toward the other end of the bar. "I'm thinking about getting back to work. Quitting while I'm ahead and all that."

Interesting. "How are you ahead?"

"Well, I haven't had to mention anything about my three older brothers and how a year later I'm still waiting for one of them to come and drag me home by the hair."

He thought of her hair loosened and draped over his skin, thought of her courage in the face of her family's expectations, thought of the long, hard career road down which she wanted to travel.

And then he wondered why he was thinking about more than bedding her.

"You remind me a lot of a girl I knew in high school." He shifted to sit more comfortably in his chair. "Her situation was different, her family nothing like yours. But she still had to make her way on her own."

"And did she succeed?"

He smiled, thinking of his two friends from Johnson High in Austin, of Heidi Malone from the wrong side of the tracks who'd played sax and become the fifth member of his band, who was now an attorney defending women's rights, thinking of her married now for six years to Ben Tannen.

"Oh, yeah." Quentin's smile widened. "She's come a long way from the waif I knew her as then."

"Really. So you have a thing for waifish schoolgirls, do you?"

He laughed aloud, the sound unfamiliar to his ears. He started to speak, was stopped by the movement of the chair beside his.

"I certainly hope he doesn't, considering the wealth of experienced fish in the sea he has to choose from."

Quentin turned into a cloud of perfume. The woman who'd sat beside him was gorgeous in that way of starlets, with perfect makeup and perfect hair, nails as bright as jewels and jewels as subtle as her plunging neckline.

She was most definitely on the make. And these days Quentin much preferred the thought of bedding tousled bartenders.

"Sweetie, would you get me a Cosmopolitan? Light on the cranberry." The woman gave her order to Shandi, then dismissed her and turned his way. "You are buying tonight, aren't you, hon? Or did I get all dressed up for nothing?"

Nothing was just about it. Not a twinge in his body.

But he smiled because that's what he did, and when Shandi returned with the woman's Cosmo, he said, "Put it on my tab."

YOU HAVE A THING FOR WAIFISH schoolgirls, do you?

Gah, had she actually asked him that? What was wrong with her? What was she thinking? Oh, wait. She wasn't thinking. A big, fat problem that seemed to be worsening as the night grew long.

Show her a gorgeous man and for some ridiculous reason she lost every bit of her mind.

Here she was, telling Quentin all the things she didn't want him to know—especially where she'd come from—giving him the ammunition he needed to deduce who she was. Who she wasn't. Who she didn't ever want to be.

And once he figured out all of that…

In the back room of the bar, Shandi rested against the wall next to the telephone and bulletin board, then beat her head against the surface almost hard enough to leave a dent.

Uh, a dent in the wall, not in her head. Her head was thick and indestructible, or so was the obvious conclusion, what with the way none of her lectures on what to say and what not to say had managed to sink in.

The phone rang in her ear. She jerked up the receiver more to kill the noise than because it was her job while Armand covered the bar. "Erotique. Shandi Fossey."

"Shan, will you kill me if I bail on tomorrow night's movie? Daddy called and insists I come for dinner, and there's no way I can get back by eight. I'm going to spend the night and return Wednesday morning."

Well, crud. Once again, April's priorities and unbreakable family ties meant Shandi would be spending her night off scrambling to find a last-minute date. "Depends. Are you taking Evan with you?"

"Don't be nuts. It's a command performance. Family only. Some ridiculous emergency about Trevor being seen in public with Stefan Navarro."

Shandi rolled her eyes. "I was wondering about that."

"About what? My brother's sexuality?"

"No. About whether or not you really considered Evan family."

"Jeez, Shan. Give it a break, will you? Evan and I are fine. And I rather like having him here all to myself."

Right. As long as you have him that way fully clothed, Shandi mused, then took it back.

Evan and April's relationship was none of her business—even though they were her two very best friends and had been since that first day after classes last year when, bleary-eyed and suffering from information overload, she and April had shared a table in the Starbucks where Evan worked as a barista.

"Fine," she grumbled. "I'll go to the show by myself."

"Well, yeah, you could." April paused strategically. "But you don't have to."

"You're not fixing me up, April. You're not, you're not, you're not. Never again in this lifetime. Understand?" Life was too short to suffer through bad blind dates.

"Trust me. I know better. Besides, I don't have to." April paused. "Evan says you've got some guy at the hotel who's dishy."

Ah, yes. The 3:30 a.m. sacred hour of confession. "He is dishy, but I don't have him. In fact, he's currently at the bar being had by a Bambi in serious need of paint thinner. You should see the layers she's troweled on."

April snorted. "Not everyone can manage the fresh-faced farm-girl look, you know. You've pretty much cornered that market."

"Uh-huh. And thanks for rubbing it in." The reminder was hardly what Shandi needed when she was doing all she could to wipe away every trace of the farm.

She wanted to fit in, not stand out. To gain attention because of her skills, not her accent and the fact that, yes, she really had ridden in barrel-racing competitions.

To prove to her family that she damn well could make it on her own. To prove the same to herself.

This time April sighed. "You know, sweetie, you really do need to get over where you come from."

"Oh, and you don't let where you come from dictate your relationship with Evan?"

"Why? Has he said something to you? Is that why you're all over us all of a sudden? What did he say? Is he complaining that I won't take him to Connecticut?"

"Evan hasn't said a word." She leaned forward to stretch out her taut and tired back. "I'm just feeling out of my league here."

"Well, stop it. You have no reason to."

"Did I tell you he's from Texas?"

"The dishy guy?"

"Yeah, he's from Austin." She straightened, then slid down the wall and sat on her heels.

"Wouldn't that be a plus in his favor? Having that similar-regional-outlook thing going on?"

"No, it's not a plus, you goon. I live here and he doesn't." What kind of plus was that? "And who said we shared any regional outlook anyhow?"

"Hmm," April hummed before saying, "So? Have fun with him here."

"Right. The kind of fun that involves not wearing anything."

April sighed, and this time with more force. "Hey, it's only a thought. It's one of many that prove you think about sex too much."

"That coming from someone who doesn't think about it at all," Shandi said, immediately wishing she could bite off her tongue. Especially when she couldn't even hear breathing on the other end of the line.

She waited one heartbeat, two. "April? Are you still there?"

"I'm here. And now I'm pissed as hell. You said Evan hadn't been talking."

"He hasn't. Not really." How much more trouble was she going to get into with her mouth? "I was talking to him about Dishy Guy, and we got into a discussion about the girls guys sleep with versus the ones they take home."

When April stayed silent, Shandi stood and went back to pounding her head on the wall. "Listen, April, my break's up. I've got to get back. Can we talk about this later?"

"I love him, Shandi. More than I knew I could love anyone." April's voice broke. "He's everything to me, and I'm scared to death I'm going to do something major to screw it up."

The noises from the bar faded into the background until Shandi heard only the hum of the back room's cooler. Guilt swelled in her chest that she'd even inadvertently betrayed a confidence.

She had a hard time swallowing around the lump of emotion clogging her throat. "You're not. Oh, April, you're not. He feels the same about you. You know that."

"Does he? I mean, I know he does, but with all this family stuff…"

Eyes closed, Shandi drew in a deep breath. "We'll talk when you get back from Connecticut, okay? After class on Wednesday. We'll come grab something fabulous at Amuse Bouche. I'm broke, and this way it's all free."

April laughed. "Sounds good. Besides, I'm sure I'll be stressed from the Daddy-Trevor-Stefan triangle and need to unload."

April rang off then, and Shandi hung up the phone, glancing briefly at the bulletin board and the huge pink pushpin tacking up a scrawled note that said:

Mrs. Mulholland told Mrs. Delancey her doctor says her BP is up, up, up!
Go light salting her margaritas!

Hopefully Shandi would be better at watching Mrs. M's salt than she'd been thus far at watching the words that came out of her own mouth. Honesty being the best policy had never before seemed like such a bad idea.

And when she stepped out of the back room and into the bar, into the conversations and the laughter and the music with the low throbbing beat, she really had to remind herself how much trouble she'd generated already today simply by speaking her mind.

Especially because right now her mind wanted to rip the arms off the painted Bambi draped all over Quentin.

"Scotch neat to the gentleman at the far end," Armand said, lightly salting the margarita glasses for the aforementioned duo of Mulholland and Delancey. He glanced at Shandi, then back at the salted rims. "Too much?"

She reached for an old-fashioned glass and the scotch. "Any less and she'll know we're onto her."

Armand screwed the top from the silver shaker and finished off the drinks while Shandi poured hers and served the customer per her coworker's instructions. She listened to Armand flirting with the two older women, grinning to herself as the teasing between the three grew boldly risqué.

She tried to remember why they were here sans husbands and wedding bands, certain she'd stored the gossip in a tiny part of her mind not overloaded with school, work, friends, family and the resulting guilt trips she took.

But right now she couldn't access any slot in her

memory banks because she'd looked up and caught Quentin's eye.

Gone was the man she'd chatted up and flirted with two nights in a row. The man who'd managed to get her to talk about herself when she never talked about herself.

The man who had been about as mellow as anyone in the entertainment industry with whom she'd crossed paths.

He wasn't mellow now.

He was holding on to his temper with a politely woven thread that was unraveling in direct proportion to Bambi's aggressive thrust of her exposed cleavage. And even Shandi, standing where she was, felt the heat of his simmering irritation.

She ignored a smugly satisfied thrill. Or at least she tried. *Round one to the long-legged filly. Bambi was on her way down.*

Time for an intervention. A fire alarm. A police action in the lobby. Janice, Hush's general manager, wouldn't be supportive should Shandi instigate either.

That left a phone call.

She stepped into the back room, reached for the phone's portable handset and punched in all but the last in the sequence of numbers for her cell. Then she took a deep breath and headed for the end of the bar where Quentin sat.

"Mr. Marks?"

His gaze snagged hers sharply. "Yes?"

"I'm sorry to interrupt—" she gave Bambi a soft smile "—but you have a phone call."

"Thanks," he said, and when he reached for the handset, she surreptitiously hit the last number and whispered, "Excuse me," to the Bambi as Quentin stepped from the bar chair to take the call.

On her way to the back room, she walked by Armand and begged him to cover her for five more minutes. In her pants pocket, her cell was already vibrating; Armand simply rolled his eyes and mouthed, "You owe me."

She answered what felt like seconds before the call rolled to voice mail. "Shandi Fossey. Bartender extraordinaire and interventionist."

In her ear Quentin laughed, a sexy throaty sound. "Where are you?"

"In the back room," she said, leaning against the same wall she'd rested on while talking to April, enjoying his voice a whole lot more than her girlfriend's.

"How do I get back there?"

"You don't. Employees only."

"You want me to just keep your phone?"

Crud. "Uh, no. The wall around the corner from the end of the bar? There's a panel door. It's hidden, but if you find and hit the button, it'll swing open."

"You're going to make me work for it then?"

It? Oh…my. "Lesson number one." Anticipation lent a sultry breathlessness to her voice. "I've never been one to make it easy on a man."

A beat of silence, then he said, "Now that I can't wait to see. Stay there."

No problem, since she couldn't move to save her soul. She listened to the phone disconnect, her heart pounding in her ears along with the lost signal's beep.

And then despite standing frozen in place, Shandi began to sweat.

3

QUENTIN FOUND THE DOOR, found the button and seconds later found himself on the opposite end of the room from where Shandi stood.

She held her cell phone pressed close between her breasts, her chest rising and falling at a rapid pace visible even from here.

Her eyes sparkled. He could see the starry flash in the flickering light cast by the one and only fixture running the length of the ceiling. He let the door close behind him slowly, let the latch click, let the echo fade away before he took his first step.

She wore a pin-tucked tuxedo shirt in a dark rosy-pink, a black satin cummerbund, bow tie and tuxedo pants, and leaned against the wall beside the main doorway leading from the back room into the bar.

She looked as if she couldn't wait for him to reach her. As if the phone's empty wall unit next to her head was just an excuse to get him alone. He held the handset tightly, his palm sweating as he approached her.

Sweating even more when the look in her eyes grew bold and warm in ways that surprised him.

He wondered what it would've been like to meet her later. Meet her in Austin. To get to know her on his own turf, his own terms, instead of in an environment where he'd long ago quit trusting anything to be real.

He wanted her to be real. He so wanted her to be real.

Shandi held out her hand. "I don't take kindly to blackmail, you know."

He didn't know. He didn't know her at all. And since he'd be leaving the city in a matter of days, he'd never have the full pleasure—a thought that caused quite the uncomfortable hitch in his chest.

"Got it," he said. "Blackmail's off-limits. Lying's on the can-do list."

"Uh-uh. I never lied." She reached for the handset he offered, but he wasn't ready to let go, and when she pulled, he followed, the momentum bringing him closer still. She arched a dark blond brow but didn't push him away. "You did have a phone call. A very conveniently timed one."

She tugged. He moved in, one more step that brought him near enough to feel the ragged breath she released. "Unless my telepathic reception was off and you weren't begging for a rescue."

Cute. Very cute. Covering her nerves with cocky bravado when at this distance he could see the sheen of perspiration on her skin.

He took the handset away from her and hung it in place without anything close to a struggle. "No. I was begging. And thank you for the save."

She shrugged, then tucked her hands behind her. "All in a day's work."

"I've heard that about your profession."

"Hey, what's a bartender for but to hear confessions and intervene on behalf of those seeking salvation?"

Salvation. Was that what drew him to her? The idea that she possessed the secret to saving him from sliding deeper into his cynical pit? "Well, you do deliver a truly religious experience."

"I aim to please."

God, but her face was amazing. Her smile wide and dimpled. Her eyes reflecting lights found nowhere in the room. Wisps of baby-fine hairs framed her face, and he found himself reaching up, smoothing several where they brushed her temple.

There were so many things he wanted to know about her, to ask, to hear her tell him in that soft Oklahoma voice. He didn't know which to ask first, and so in the end he said nothing. He simply stroked the bare shell of her ear.

"You're staring, Quentin," she said, her voice a whisper.

He blinked, pulled his hand away, clenched his fingers. Most women visibly preened beneath his stare. Shandi's soft accusation intrigued him almost as much as the hint of a blush on her cheeks.

"So," he began, backing a step away, needing even that little bit of distance in order to avoid seeming as if he was only here to get his hands on her. "What's next?"

She crossed her arms over her chest, a move more protective than defensive. "What do you mean?"

He nodded in the direction of the bar. "I'm assuming you need to get back to work."

"I do," she said almost in relief.

"And I can't stay here forever."

"You can't."

"And if Mrs. Cyprus is still drinking me into the poorhouse," he added with a pained grin, "I'm not going back out there."

Shandi held up one finger and pushed open the bar door far enough to look out. When she stepped back, two impish dimples belied her somber tone. "She is. Though I will be sure to tell her you've settled your tab with regrets."

What he was regretting was that tonight's time with Shandi was coming to an end. That he hadn't yet managed to throw out a great line that would reel her in.

He'd been the pursued, the proverbial trophy for so many years that he couldn't even remember how to bait a damn hook—proving again how very much he needed this change in his life.

And then Shandi asked, "Do you ever get used to it?"

"Used to what?"

"The groupies? The fame hunters? Whatever you call them?"

So now she was a mind reader, too? Unbelievable. "If you mean the I'll-stroke-yours-if-you'll-stroke-mine come-ons, then yeah. I'm used to it." He took the admission further. "These days I'm surprised when it doesn't happen."

He'd grown used to women's scrutiny; it came with

the job and the looks, and there had been a time he'd embraced the attention for the perk it was.

But he was long past that place in his life, past taking advantage of offers or free glasses of wine, past welcoming the advances, past defining his success by how often he was recognized.

"And here I was just thinking how lucky you are to have turned your passion into a successful career."

He liked that she'd been thinking of him. But the last thing he wanted to inspire in her was sympathy. He shoved his hands in his pockets and shrugged. "Look, I'll be in the city till the first of next week. I'd like to see you away from the bar. Hell, away from the hotel."

She pursed her lips into a bow while thinking over his suggestion. "I'm off tomorrow night. And—" she gestured toward the phone "—I was just stood up for a movie date."

He grinned. "I'm a huge movie fan."

She laughed, a crystal clear sound that tickled like wind chimes. "Is that so? Not even knowing what I was going to see?"

"Doesn't matter. I'm more interested in the company."

"Okay then," she said after only a moment's hesitation. "The theater's only a few blocks from here. You want to meet in the lobby at seven?"

"Sounds like a plan."

"Super." She clasped her hands together. "I'd, uh, better get back before Armand drags me back by my hair."

He smiled. "Before you go?"

She arched both brows, nodded.

"Is there another way out of here so I don't have to sneak out through the bar?"

"C'mon. I'll take you out through the kitchen. Chef is pretty famous in his own right, so he'll totally understand wanting to avoid the groupies."

Quentin turned to follow her through the swinging doors at the rear of the room, the same lightness in his step that he'd noticed after making the decision to return to Texas.

He wasn't sure if that was a good thing or bad and quite frankly right now he didn't give a damn.

SHANDI RIPPED THE YELLOW long-sleeved silk T-shirt over her head and tossed it to the floor on top of the cropped black jeans, the denim corset dress, the rose-colored ruffle-front blouse and at least four other similarly inappropriate outfits.

Evan, who'd been sitting on the foot of her bed, collapsed onto the mattress with an exasperated groan. "Why am I here, Shandi? Why the hell am I even here?"

She plodded out from behind her room divider, a silk screen of Mae West prints. Wearing her ratty chenille bathrobe, she dropped to sit on the hardwood floor in the middle of all the clothes.

"You're here because A, you have nothing better to do, B, April can't be here and C, I happen to trust your taste and I need the opinion of an eye other than my own."

"I'm gouging mine out now, so you're SOL."

She picked up a lime leather miniskirt and threw it at him. "And you call yourself a roommate."

"I call myself male, and I come with the requisite lack of fashion sense."

"Or—so the rumor goes—you don't come at all."

Evan levered himself up onto his elbows again. "Is that a reference to my love life? Because I can assure you that the rumor is wrong."

"Been taking matters into your own hands again?"

"As often as possible."

Shandi laughed but stopped short of admitting she shared his pain. Her love life of late was nonexistent and her sex life a figment of her fantasies, her hands and one or two very special battery-operated boyfriends.

She sighed. "If I were going out with you or April, I wouldn't be having this problem, you know."

"Right. April and I don't rate."

"It's not that and you know it. It's just that with the two of you I can be myself."

Evan heaved an enormous sigh. "This may come as a big shock, Shandi, but guys like women comfortable enough to be themselves."

"I know."

"Then be yourself. I can't imagine any hetero guy with half a brain and at least one good eye not being attracted to you."

Aww, he was so cute with his compliments…or maybe not! "Now I see why April is so crazy about you. You are one amazing sweet-talker, Evan Harcourt."

"Shandi, shut the hell up and get dressed."

"Easy for you to say. You're not the one trying to be yourself without sending a member of the opposite sex screaming into the night." Willowy cat's tail of a filly. Long, tall drink of whiskey and water. Uh-uh. Not tonight.

"Woman," Evan said with a growl, "I'm about to kick your whiny ass back to Oklahoma."

"That's it. As The Donald would say, you're fired. I'll just do this on my own."

"Best news I've heard all night." He smacked his palms to his thighs, pushed up from her bed and stood. "Just no blaming me if anything goes wrong."

"How can it go wrong?" She gave him a narrow glare. "I'm what every half-witted, one-eyed man wants."

"And on that extra whiny note, I'm gone."

"Fine." She stuck out her tongue, then collapsed onto her back in the mountain of clothes and stared at the ceiling.

She was being childish and she knew it, but stress tended to do that to her. She grew pouty and petulant and always felt better after pitching a fit.

But now it was time to get over it. She sat up and thought about Quentin—what she knew of him, what she hadn't yet learned, what different impression she might make as his date than she already had as his bartender.

It was time to turn the heat up a notch. But how?

It was when her gaze landed on the short green-and-blue-plaid skirt hanging in her closet that she knew exactly. Ooh, but she loved it when a plan came together!

You have a thing for waifish schoolgirls, do you?

"I THINK I STARTED SINGING in front of audiences as soon as I learned to talk."

It was Tuesday night, nearing seven o'clock. Quentin was sitting in the elegant boutique hotel's art-deco lobby, relaxing back in one of the plush leather chairs, waiting for Shandi. At least, he was sitting and he was waiting.

The relaxing part had ceased the minute Mrs. Cyprus had sat down in the chair beside him and opened her mouth. She had yet to shut it.

"In grade school, I actually sang the lead in *Annie*. Can you believe it? I wasn't even ten years old and I won the part over children older than I was."

This was what Shandi had saved him from last night, what he wished she would show up and save him from now. Sure, he could save himself by heading to one of the lobby shops, the restaurant or the bar, even back to his room.

But he had this thing about wanting to be right here to see Shandi walk through the front door. To see her before she saw him. He liked catching her unawares, wanting to weigh the expression on her face as she sought him out. Doing so might not tell him a thing, he mused, frowning as he watched a huge black cat stroll through the lobby, but he wanted those few brief moments anyway.

"The summer before my freshman year in high school was when I caught the notice of my camp counselors. I organized a routine for my backup dancers and sang a medley of Elvis songs. You should've seen our costumes."

He nodded, smiled, then braced his elbows on the chair arms and laced his fingers, tapped his thumbs to his chin. He wasn't going to give up what he wanted more than anything right now because of the annoying woman at his side reciting her résumé.

He simply tuned her out, shut down the volume, left her running as background noise. Funny how adept he'd become at ignoring what he didn't want to hear. And how often he had to stop and wonder if he was tuning out what he shouldn't.

If he was paying attention when he should.

If he'd become too jaded to recognize the difference.

"I studied voice at university. Oh, the raves over my performances. It was the sort of reaction I'd been working toward all my life. And I knew I was on my way. That I'd never get enough."

She might not have gotten enough, but this one-sided conversation was edging close to more than he was willing to put up with. And he'd just moved his hands to the chair arms to push himself up and make his excuses when the revolving glass doors swung around and there Shandi was.

Or so he first thought. It took a second glance and then a very long and lingering third before he was able to convince himself he was seeing Shandi and not a young girl at whom he shouldn't be staring at all.

At his side Mrs. Cyprus continued to chatter, remaining oblivious to everything but herself. And that gave Quentin the freedom to focus.

He started at Shandi's feet, where she wore penny loafers and white kneesocks, both of the sort he hadn't seen on girls since grade school. And never on a woman he wanted to bed the way he wanted to bed this one. He felt like a complete perv and loved the thrum of arousal stirring in his groin.

He followed the long lines of her legs where they disappeared beneath a green-and-blue-plaid skirt so short it barely covered her ass. And from this vantage point, sitting lower than her hemline, that coverage was questionable.

He was able to see skin and curves and what appeared to be an edge of frilly white lace that had his gut tightening like that of a starving man.

His gaze had reached her white blouse—gauzy and nearly sheer—when she finally saw him. She turned and headed his way, and he sat immobile and watched the gorgeous bounce and sway of her braless breasts.

When she lifted a hand to her mouth, he followed the movement and watched her pull a red lollipop from between her lips. This time it was more than his gut that clenched and stirred, and he shifted in his seat to calm the buzz threatening to turn into full-tilt arousal.

Little good it did. Especially once he got a good look at her hair worn in pigtails. And at her face.

Her skin was made up to appear as translucent as pale porcelain yet soft and warm instead of fragile. Her lips and cheeks were tinted pink, a shade he only saw when she tilted her head and smiled and the light picked up the shimmer.

But, oh god, her eyes. He'd seen stage makeup. He'd seen exotic costuming. Hell, working in music videos, he'd seen it all—or so he'd thought, because he didn't think he'd ever seen eyes like Shandi's at any time in his life.

And it wasn't just the way she'd used the cobalt- and violet-blues, the greens that seemed to reflect every hue between teal and jade. It was the way she'd used her face as a canvas. From her brows to her temples to her cheekbones.

The end result of the application of makeup resembled a colorfully jeweled Mardi Gras mask, complete with hints of ruby and gold. Except there was no mask. It was all done with the tools of her trade.

But the biggest impact, the one striking him like a blow in the chest, came from her expression. The look in her eyes. The way she was looking at him.

He couldn't help it. He slid deeper into his seat, sat on his spine, spread his legs and groaned.

"I just know there's an audience waiting out there for my voice, for the way I make every song my own…excuse me?" Mrs. Cyprus looked up as Shandi stepped between Quentin's knees. "This is a private conversation."

"Oh, don't mind me." Shandi sidled closer, fluffing her skirt before sitting down in his lap, her weight on his thigh as her free hand went around his neck. "My bedtime story can wait until you grown-ups are done."

Quentin chuckled as Shandi crossed her legs. He brought one hand down behind her to hold her hip in place and draped his other arm over her knees. Now that he had her where he wanted her, he was not about to let her go.

He cleared his throat lightly, trying not to grin. "Mrs. Cyprus has been sharing her fascinating experiences in musical theater."

"Ooh, can I stay and listen?" Shandi asked. "I know it's late, but I promise to go to bed the minute you tell me to if I can hear one story. Please?"

"Just one then," he said, his hand slipping to the hem of her skirt and finding the lacy edge of her panties exposed. "As long as Mrs. Cyprus doesn't mind. She was telling me how she's performed everything from *Annie* to Elvis."

"Ooh." Shandi squealed as she waved her lollipop. "I love *Annie*. Can you sing it for me? That song about tomorrow?"

When Mrs. Cyprus looked from Shandi and met Quentin's gaze, he simply shrugged and tried to appear chagrined—not an easy task with his body tight enough to snap. She got to her feet, smoothed down her slacks and the halter vest that exposed even more than her plunging neckline last night.

"I'm sorry to have wasted your time," she said to Quentin. "But not half as sorry as I am to have wasted mine. Had I known you preferred girls to women…"

She left the sentence unfinished and then left the lobby, heading into the bar. Quentin watched Shandi watch the other woman go, finally finding enough of his voice to ask, "Do you think she recognized you?"

"Are you kidding?" Shandi huffed, gestured with the candy. "To recognize me she would have had to actually look at me when she ordered her drinks. Trust me. She's only had eyes for Armand. And, well, for you. But then, don't we all?"

And at that she turned her gaze on him.

God, but he hoped she was ready for what she was asking from him. Ready for what he wanted from her. He wasn't twenty years old and he was no longer in the habit of sleeping with every woman who asked.

Sex, when he engaged, was now about a need deeper than the physical. Not every woman got that. But then he intuitively knew that Shandi Fossey was not every woman.

He left his hand where it was at the hem of her skirt. "Are we going to be late for the movie?"

"I was thinking about that." She popped the sucker in her mouth, popped it out, shifted a bit so that his hand contacted skin as well as lace. "I'm not sure I want to wear this to the theater."

Meaning she'd dressed for him and not their date? "You want to change first?"

She shook her head, threaded her fingers into his hair. "There's not enough time before the movie starts."

He tightened his hold on her knees. "Dinner then? Drinks?"

She considered him closely while loosening the band holding his hair. It took him several endless moments while he fought down an erection to realize they were still sitting in the hotel lobby, that around them people came and went, that not a soul seemed to notice—or care—how intimately they sat embraced.

Shandi seemed perfectly comfortable, and he strangely enough didn't feel one bit ill at ease. Whether it was the ambience of the hotel or their connection, he couldn't say.

As long as she stayed right where she was, it really didn't matter. He just didn't want her to move.

"We could do dinner or drinks, sure," she finally said. "Or we could go to the library."

She wanted to go to the library? "Is it even open this late?"

She laughed. "Oh, not the public library. The one upstairs."

The Hush library. Admittedly more interesting. "You're serious then."

"About?"

Her fingers massaged the base of his skull, and it was all he could do not to close his eyes and let her have at him right here and now. "About a bedtime story."

"Well, we don't have to be in a bed."

There was no other place he wanted to be. And he started to say so.

But Shandi stopped him by whispering close to his ear, "There are enough sofas and chairs in the library to make you forget you ever needed a bed for anything."

4

THE ELEVATOR RIDE UP DROVE her mad.

She and Quentin both stood against the back of the car, side by side, hands curled over the railing at their hips, not touching, not speaking, simply letting the ascent heighten the tension that sang in the air.

She stared at their reflections mirrored on the stainless-steel doors. Her skirt appeared the size of a bandage, her legs the length of fence posts. The colorful mask with which she'd taken exquisite care looked like a neon bar sign. Her pigtails like commas of corn on the cob.

Oh, yeah. She was definitely this man's type. *Mr. Sophistication? Meet Clueless in Manhattan.* She wanted to slam her palm against the panel of buttons and stop this joke of a journey.

Stop it, put the car in reverse, back her way into the lobby and out into the street. She wanted to start over. To meet Quentin Marks on a level playing field. Not on one where she felt like a rube.

But then it was too late. The doors slid open with a whisper. He gestured for her to precede him, and she did, turning toward the double glass doors that separated the airy room that was their destination from the hallway.

He walked far enough behind that she couldn't see him without turning, that she couldn't touch him without reaching out. Close enough that she could feel that he was there, hovering without threatening, looming without alarming, beguiling and tempting and hot.

At the entrance Quentin reached for the handle and pulled open the door. Shandi stepped through, dropped her lollipop into a wastebasket. The room was empty, the only light that of several reading lamps left burning low.

The sky outside glowed with the hues of the sunset, and the walls of windows had begun to reflect the room, the atmosphere one of the kind of intimacy found only after dark. She stopped as Quentin joined her and as the door eased shut.

"This," she said with a sweep of one hand, "is the library. The sofas and armchairs I mentioned, along with everything from classics to erotica to popular fiction." Breathing deeply of the room's bound leather and wood, deeply of the subtle scent of the man behind her, Shandi moved farther into the room. "Pick your poison."

He walked ahead of her, stopping to study the space and giving her a full rear view of his body. So far she'd seen him sitting down at the bar and in the lobby. She'd had a full-frontal view, too, when he'd come toward her in Erotique's back room. But, oh, did she like seeing him from here.

His shoulders were broad, his waist narrow, his backside taut beneath the expensive fabric of his dress pants. His hair was the mane she'd described it as. Leonine as it hung there in waves of gold and tawny-brown resting on the tops of his shoulder blades. It was thick and beautiful, and he wore it as few men could.

And then he turned and met her gaze. His brows came down. A wickedly sexy V. "I'll pick the chair. You pick the story."

She laced her hands at her back, hooked one foot behind the other, canted her head to the side and rocked back and forth, playing up the part she'd created. "Where do you want me to sit?"

"In my lap, of course," he said and reached out, pulled her hand from behind her and led her across the room to the far corner. The chair he chose was built for two, not quite the size of a love seat but definitely not meant for a single. He turned and dropped into it, tugging her down.

She sat sideways in his lap, her back against the plush arm that was wider than her body. Her feet she settled on the cushion on Quentin's far side, where there would've been plenty of room for her to sit if he'd let her.

He hadn't. He didn't. He wouldn't.

Instead he draped one arm over her bare thighs, one behind her on the arm of the chair. He was so close. Right there. Inches away. It was hard to breathe, to think, to believe she was sitting in the lap of a man with this one's fame, fortune and reputation.

With this one's trail of broken hearts...because she was sure they must be legion.

"So what story do you want to hear?" he asked softly, his fingers toying with the end of one of her pigtails. He gestured toward the stack of books on the side table. "Beck Desmond? Harlan Coben? Charles Dickens? Anaïs Nin?"

Shandi shook her head. There was only one story she wanted. "Quentin Marks. I want to know everything. From his humble roots to his rise to stardom. And all the juicy bits in between."

His mouth crooked. A dimple appeared at the edge of his beard stubble. "That story will put you right to sleep. I was hoping to keep you awake. At least for a little while."

She had no intention of falling asleep now any more than she had of *staying* asleep on Christmas morning. Not with this gift she'd been given, this man who'd come out of nowhere and into her life when she'd least expected anyone to arrive.

She looked away from his gaze that left her breathless—oh, but his scotch-and-water eyes were compelling—to where she held her fingers twined together against what there was of her skirt. That didn't help much with distracting her since his arm lay across her thighs.

Thankfully it wasn't his skin but the fine fabric of his dress shirt she felt there. Otherwise she was quite sure she wouldn't have been able to speak. "I doubt anything you could tell me would put me to sleep."

"Trust me. I'm as boring as it gets."

"I don't believe it. I've read enough about you in *Peo-*

ple and *Vanity Fair* to know how fascinating you are."
When he gave a soft snort, she smiled, cast him a quick
glance and laughingly added, "Hey, it's better than reading what all the tabloids have to say."

He used his arm across her thighs to pull her closer.
"Too bad all of the music-loving public doesn't share
your restraint. Or your taste in publications."

She couldn't help it. She had to tease, to take her
mind off what his fingers were doing to her leg. "Those
paternity suits getting to you, are they?"

He groaned, shook his head. "You'd think I wouldn't
be surprised after what I've seen, but that one left me
reeling. The lengths people go to, thinking they can
shortcut the process."

"Lengths like regaling you with their curriculum
vitae and cleavage in a hotel lobby?" she asked, thinking of Mrs. Cyprus.

"Yeah." He chuckled. "Lengths like that."

"Or like dressing up in schoolgirl plaid and kneesocks and begging for a story?" she asked, wondering
if he thought her desperate and waiting several long
heartbeats for him to answer.

When he finally did, it wasn't what she wanted to
hear. "Look at me, Shandi."

She didn't want to look at him because she was already feeling all itchy and hot being in his lap, and it
was not a part of the evening's plans to make a fool of
herself. At least, no more than she could help.

But he was waiting patiently in that way that seemed
so natural to him, and so she finally did, cutting him off

at the pass. "If I've come across that way, I haven't meant to. I'd hate to have given you that impression. That you've jumped from the frying pan of Mrs. Cyprus into my fire."

"I've never felt your spending time with me was because of what I can do for you professionally." He raised his arm from her lap, stroked his knuckles over her cheek, his persuasive gaze holding hers spellbound. "If it is, then you're a better actress than those who've offered to exchange, uh, favors. Either that, or I'm blinded by infatuation."

"Oh, please." Her heart tripping wildly, she dropped her gaze, feeling strangely shy and out of her league. She reached over to toy with the buttons on his shirt. "Infatuation my ass. You just like the way I mix your drinks."

"I like a lot of things about you. And, yeah, a couple of them do involve the bar." He returned his arm to her lap, used his hand on her hip barely covered by her excuse for a skirt to scoop her close. "You see, when I'm sitting there in that chair at the end, I can watch you work."

She slipped a finger between two of the buttons on his shirt placket, tickled by his thatch of soft hair she found beneath. "You like watching me work?"

"I like watching you move." When she slipped a button through its hole, his breath caught. When she slipped a second, he exhaled. When she slipped a third, he sank deeper into the chair and grinned. "Your legs are absolutely amazing."

She found herself twisting up her mouth to keep from grinning along. "Isn't that a rather boorish attempt at a compliment?"

"No doubt," he said with a low, husky laugh. "But since we're both being honest…"

"Honest?" she asked, opening his shirt and slipping her fingers along his collarbone, absorbing the warmth of his skin. "About what?"

"You're undressing me." His palm spanned the back of her thigh; his thumb stroked along the leg of her white lace panties. "I'm assuming the attraction is mutual."

"It is," she admitted, even as Evan's words came back to haunt her. Did she want to be another woman-notch on Quentin's bedpost? Or did she have her sights set on being the one he took home with him to Austin?

The first was fine, she decided, since he would be the biggest man-notch she'd ever made; the second wasn't a possibility she'd even consider. She had no intention of making her life anywhere other than exactly where she was.

Still, she couldn't help but be curious. What in the world would a man like Quentin Marks want with her?

She suppressed a shiver, her belly tingling with the ebb and flow of her nerves. "It's as mutual as it gets. As long as you're not here *only* because of my legs."

"Not a chance. Legs I can get anywhere," he said, and she brought her gaze back to his, arching her brow and drawing a gravelly chuckle. "I like your ambition a lot, Shandi. That you don't think of success as your right and expect it to be handed to you."

"Well, no. Putting in long hours to get what you want is pretty much a way of life in Round-Up," she said, wanting to kick herself the minute the words left her mouth. Now all he'd be seeing was the long-legged, willowy cat's tail of a filly she was trying so hard to be so much more than.

Except he didn't say a thing about Round-Up. He simply went on. "I also like that you're determined *and* realistic about fighting the odds. You wouldn't believe how many think the business is solely about the very necessary connections. They forget the hard work or refuse to face the reality that they might never have what it takes."

She pressed the pad of her thumb to his pulse where it popped at the base of his throat, feeling the contraction of his muscles there when he swallowed and fighting the urge to slip out of her panties and straddle his lap. "The first I won't argue with. The second? That's harder. Especially if accepting that reality means giving up a dream."

He didn't respond immediately. He simply sat there, his heart beating, his chest rising and falling, his skin warm against her wrist, finally asking, "Are you calling me a cynical bastard?"

"No," she said, raising her gaze from the relief map of tendons and veins and muscles in his neck to meet his eyes, heavy lidded and sharp. "I think that's what you're calling yourself."

"Does that bother you?" he asked, his gaze dropping to her mouth, where she'd caught her lower lip between her teeth. "The fact that I don't share your optimism?"

She moved her fingertips from his throat to his chin and to his mouth, where her thumb stroked over the pillow of his bottom lip. "Not enough to make me keep my clothes on."

"The best news I've heard all night," he said, cupping the back of her head and pulling her down for a kiss, pressing his mouth to hers, his tongue to the seam of her lips, seeking the same entry here she wanted to give him elsewhere.

She turned and leaned into his chest, wanting this more than she'd ever wanted anything from a man. His bitterness made her heart ache. His body, his smile—both made her knees go weak. The questions in his eyes made her mind race with ways to answer his challenge.

But right now what he made her was pins-and-needles aware. His hand slid farther beneath her skirt, his fingers finding the elastic of her panties and easing underneath. She parted her legs, whimpering into his mouth when he found how wet she was, when he pushed one finger inside her.

Cupping his cheek, she kissed him, clenching her sex around his teasing, probing finger while sliding her tongue the length of his, stroking, nibbling, tasting him and testing the edges of his teeth. And when his questing thumb found the bud of her clit, she did what she'd been waiting to do.

She reached between their bodies, between his legs, found the base of his shaft that was thickly erect and squeezed. He tore his mouth from hers. "You keep that up, story hour will be over and it will be time for bed," he said in a near feral growl.

The way he said it, the desperate echo of restraint in his whisper, the desire that spilled swollen from his pores…she could hardly think, hardly breathe. She was desperate to take him, to feel him, to have him thick and hot and pulsing inside.

"What did I tell you when we came up here?" she asked, struggling to find her voice. "About the sofas and chairs and not needing a bed?"

This time the sound he made was that of a man tortured. He pulled his hand from her panties to squeeze one cheek of her ass. "Here. Now. Is that what you're saying? Is that what you want?"

"What do you want?" she asked, holding his gaze as she stroked him through the richly textured linen of his pants.

"You straddling my lap, for one thing," he said, tugging at her leg and giving her little choice. She straightened where she was sitting, climbed up and around and settled where he wanted her, her knees sinking into the seat cushion on cither side of his hips.

"Anything else?" she asked, his erection pressing like a brand against the inside of her thigh. She felt the heat through the fabric of his pants; the rigid proof of his desire amplified her own.

He settled his hands beneath her skirt at her hips and held her. "If you want to finish with my shirt buttons and start on my pants, I could go for that, too."

He wasn't the only one, she mused, pulling his shirt-tails free. Once the final button was unfastened, she parted the two sides of the garment, taking her fill of his tight abs and the trail of hair that started at his sternum and ran down behind his belt.

She followed it with her finger, watching his muscles bunch and flex as she made her way south, looking back up to see his throat convulse as he swallowed, to see his jaw set tight and hard once he had. "You like?"

"You're killing me here, Shandi," he said, grinding out the words, then pressed his lips together, his eyelids drifting down. He slid his thumbs deeper into the crease where her thigh met her hip, and she went to work on his belt, stopping only long enough to ask, "Do you have a condom?"

He nodded once, nudged away her leg to reach into his front pocket. He pulled out a money clip with a strip of three condoms tucked inside. When she arched a brow, he laughed and said, "I keep all my valuables together."

"I guess that's a good thing," she replied and freed his belt from its buckle before easing his zipper over the roadblock in the way. He wore designer boxer briefs, white, that left nothing to the imagination. She could see the bulge of veins in his shaft, the seamed ridge of his cock's plump head.

He was full and, as evidenced by the circle of moisture he'd already released, beyond ready to burst. Yet he slouched back on his spine like an expert in debauchery, all tanned and toned and king-of-the-jungle, with his scotch-and-water eyes and leonine mane.

She wanted to reach beneath the elastic, to take him in her hand and set him free. But she could not get enough of the way he looked. Her gaze drifted from the band of his boxers, tightly smooth against his abs, up that tempting line of hair bisecting his torso, to his pecs and the dark flat disks of his nipples.

She'd known men who considered themselves sex gods or a divine gift to womankind. This one lived the part. And here she was, Shandi Fossey, a bartender from Round-Up, Oklahoma, sitting in his nearly naked lap.

She glanced at the money clip he'd set on the chair arm. "Do you think we'll need more than those three?"

"I'll put in a call to room service as soon as we get back to my room," he said, moving his hands away from her hips to the buttons of her blouse.

His room. A bed. Tangled limbs on soft Egyptian cotton. Space to stretch out. To lie beneath him and feel his weight. To climb on top and ride. She closed her eyes as he unbuttoned her, shivering as she felt both the cool brush of air on her skin and the hot touch of his fingers.

He left her blouse hanging open but did not expose her the way she'd exposed him. Instead he eased his hands beneath the fabric, ran his palms up her torso to her breasts, where he cupped her, squeezed her, pinched her nipples tightly between his forefingers and thumbs.

Moaning, she leaned forward, her hands on his rib cage supporting her weight. "Do you have any idea how wonderful that feels?"

"How's this?" he asked, one hand sliding around to

her back as he crunched his gorgeous abs to sit forward and take her into his mouth. He rolled her taut nipple with his tongue, sucked her between his lips, caught her with his teeth, biting just hard enough to let her know he was there.

As if she didn't know. As if she wasn't one hundred percent in the moment.

"Mmm. That's *sooo* good," she assured him, digging the heels of her palms into his pecs and massaging him. He growled his pleasure, moved his mouth to her other breast, moved the hand still at her hip down between her legs.

Eyes still closed, she let her head fall back and tried to breathe. Impossible, what with his hand pulling aside her panties, his thumb slipping between the lips of her sex to find the bud of her clit, his palm cupping her, one finger pushing inside to stroke her.

She was a mess, wet and aroused and so very ready to come. She just didn't want to, not quite yet. Not until she'd felt that first breach of his cock's head as he entered her, that long slide as she swallowed the length of his shaft, that grinding pressure against her.

And so she wiggled on his lap and reached for his money clip, bracing her forearms on his shoulders as she tore a condom packet from the strip. Quentin let her go and sat back, slumping further into the chair's plush cushions, his grin speaking volumes.

She handed him the condom and went to work lifting him out of his shorts. He was gorgeous, the head of his cock full and ripe, an extralarge strawberry she wanted to feel on her tongue. His balls were heavy in her hand when she held them, rolled them, used an index finger to separate them.

He hissed in a breath. "I promise…we'll take our time later and do this right."

Legs spread, she settled her hands on his knees and watched as he rolled the protection into place, her skin tingling. "There's nothing wrong about doing it here and now. But, yeah, I like the idea of going back for seconds. Maybe even thirds."

"Greedy wench," he said, shoving her skirt above her hips, pulling the crotch of her panties aside. A shudder ran the length of his body, and he stroked a finger over the bare lips of her sex. "You're beautiful, do you know that?"

She sat still while he touched her, while he studied her the way he would a work of art. The thrill that ran through her was impossible to ignore. She tried. Truly, she tried; weren't all men reduced to mush by a little pink flesh?

But his appreciation seemed much more than that of a savage rutting beast and was hard not to take to heart. "You're just horny. You'd say anything to get your way."

"Ah, but that's where you're wrong," he said, lifting his gaze to hers. "If you didn't want this, then I'd chalk it up as a good time and kiss you good-night."

"But since I do…" She took hold of his erection and guided him into place.

Raising up on her knees, she pulled nothing but the head inside, not moving but to flex around him, holding his gaze as she did, as her thighs quivered, as her belly clenched, as her entire body started to shake.

She slid down slowly until he filled her, until she thought she wouldn't be able to move. Her hands on his knees again, she dropped her gaze when he did to that place where their bodies were joined.

He stretched her open where he'd entered her; so tight was the fit that she felt the throbbing of his blood as it pulsed through his veins. He dropped his head against the chair, closed his eyes as if seeking control.

When he looked back, she knew he'd lost the battle. His eyes flashed with an inner fire to match her own.

"Are you ready?" he asked, his voice low and throaty, his words only audible because of how close she sat.

She wanted to tell him she'd been ready for a lifetime, that she'd been waiting to feel this way more years than she could count. Instead she pushed forward, braced her forearms on his shoulders and opened her mouth over his.

She kissed him. Not long, wet thrusts of her tongue but a desperate connection of her lips with his. They breathed in tandem, his ragged exhalations moist against her cheek.

Their bodies moved, his up, hers down, hers up, his down, until the thrusting, driving force was the only thing that mattered. He was everywhere she needed him to be, touching places she hadn't known existed. Places in her body, but others, too…pushing her toward tears she refused to shed.

It was all too much, overwhelming, a spiraling of

sensation that quickly took her apart. She pulled her mouth from his and cried out, shuddering as her orgasm swept through her in wave after wave.

His own release followed. She felt the warmth through the layer of protection between them, felt the contraction of his muscles beneath her legs as he pulsed and pushed upward, felt the vibrating echo as he grunted, emptying himself fully, coming back down and bringing her along.

She collapsed against his chest and he held her close, his chest heaving beneath her, his skin damp against her own. His hair there tickled her breasts where she rested. His breath fluttered flyaway strands at her temple.

When she sighed, he held her tighter. When he sighed, she cuddled close.

And when he softly kissed her forehead, she knew what they'd done here had gone way beyond the simple notching of bedposts. Or the pleasurable mating of bodies. This was deeply complicated. It confused her, puzzled her.

Not to mention scared her half to death.

5

EVAN HARCOURT STOOD FACING the floor-to-ceiling windows in the sixth-floor apartment he shared with Shandi, wondering what the hell about it she found so riveting that she could sit here for hours and stare at the sky.

He saw nothing special. The tops of buildings. Satellite dishes. The last rays of the setting sun. He sure didn't see the meaning of life, the way Shandi seemed to. Maybe growing up here was the difference. He'd been looking at this same sky for twenty-six years.

If he wanted to get more out of the exercise, he might need to take up stargazing from the back porch of Shandi's family home in Round-Up. Yeah. Getting away from New York sounded like a plan. Except the family home he wanted to visit wasn't in Oklahoma.

It was in Connecticut.

He was getting tired of April putting him off. About meeting her family. About making things permanent. About sex, yeah. But that wasn't the biggest part. He'd been honest when he'd admitted to Shandi that he didn't mind waiting, that he didn't want to mess up what he was building with April.

The biggest part was the way he was beginning to wonder what he was doing making all the compromises. April was calling the shots, and like a putz, he was letting her. And the *worst* part was how long it had taken him to realize they'd reached that point.

His grandmother would kick his ass if she got wind of his situation. Ellen Harcourt had been the one to raise him after his parents had split and both proved unfit. She'd taught him the value and rewards of hard work, the importance of autonomy—financial as well as emotional.

Then again, his grandmother had been a widow and real estate mogul for forty of her sixty-eight years. And he was pretty damn sure her marriage had not been a match made from anything resembling love, lust or even like.

She'd passed her harsh outlook on to his father, who'd chosen an equally unsatisfying mate in his mother. It was a miracle, considering, that Evan had turned out as well-adjusted as he had. Wanting a real relationship. Wanting that relationship to be free of family interference. Wanting his woman to build her life with him—not a state away.

Leaning his butt against the back of the sofa, he pulled his phone from his hip and dialed April's cell. He didn't care what supposed family emergency her father had cooked up to get her to Connecticut. He needed to talk to her, to hear her voice.

When she picked up, he heard the chatter of a large gathering and his stomach clenched with the desire to be fully involved in April's life. If they were going to be together, then they needed to be together, damn it.

"Hold on a minute, Evan," she said, and he heard her making excuses in the background to her family.

He pushed off the sofa, walked across the decklike platform separating the sunken living area from the windows and the balcony. He was standing inches from the glass when she came back on the line.

"Okay, I'm here. Sorry. It's too loud at the table to hear anyone else when my father is talking, which he has been doing a lot of tonight. What's up?"

"When are you coming home?" he asked, though they'd discussed her plans earlier in the day. Problem now was that her plans were interfering with his needing to be with her, to get this crap he was feeling settled.

"In the morning. I told you. I don't have a class until ten, so I'll catch an early train." She paused, added, "Is that all you called for?"

He shoved his free hand into the pocket of his khaki Dockers. "Is there any way you can get back tonight?"

"Evan, what's wrong?" Her voice came out breathless, panicked. "Has something happened? Are you okay?"

"I'm fine." He should hang up now. He'd been stupid to call. "It's just weird not having you here when I have the night off from work."

"I know. I wish I was there. I'd told Shandi I'd see a movie with her, but I'd much rather cuddle up and watch bad reruns with you."

"Then come home tonight."

"I can't. Daddy wants—"

"I don't care what your daddy wants, April." *Goddamn.* He was not going to be a second fiddle in her life. "I care about you and me."

"Evan! What is wrong with you?"

He sighed, rubbed a hand over his forehead, listened to April breathe, heard her block the mouthpiece to respond to a question.

This wasn't the time to be having this conversation. Not when she was distracted and when he was being a shit. "Never mind. We can talk tomorrow."

"If you're going to be like that about Daddy, I don't know if I want to talk."

He jerked his hand from his pocket, slammed the heel of his palm into one of the window's wooden frames. "And if you're going to spend your life at his beck and call, then we don't have anything to talk about."

He ended the call before she could answer, turned off his phone and holstered it. She'd call back. And then she'd try the house phone. That was how she was, needing to have the last word, wanting to leave him hanging. She'd hate getting his voice mail. But not as much as he hated getting involved in her mind games.

Even though he thought Shandi's reasons weird, he'd always liked that she was making her way on her own. For the most part, he was doing the same. The only living relative he had was his grandmother, and the idea of one day being a part of April's family meant a lot to him.

Thing was, she didn't seem to understand that. She thought she could continue to string him along while doing her daddy's bidding. He shook his head, pushed away from the window, grabbed his keys off the bar separating the kitchen and the entryway and headed out.

He wasn't having any of it. April's divided loyalties had been weighing heavily for a while, but seeing Shandi's excitement earlier over this guy she didn't even know.... He hit the elevator button, hung his head while he waited.

He wanted that from April. He wanted her to be that excited about seeing him, talking to him, being with him whether they stayed in or went out. Hell, he got that excited about her. She was the sweetest thing he'd ever known. Being with her made everything about his life work.

He couldn't think of a better time than when they were together, even if they were doing nothing but watching TV or studying silently. He loved her, she loved him. He knew that—even if she jumped whenever her father snapped his fingers.

And it wasn't that he wanted her to jump for him. All he wanted was to be the number-one man in her life the same way she was the number-one woman in his.

QUENTIN WASN'T A STRANGER to women giving him anything he wanted when he took them to bed. Rarely did they demand their due. Rarely did they demand much of anything.

They faked their way through their orgasms, choked

their way through his, pretended they couldn't get enough when it wasn't him they wanted to buy. They were in the market for his contacts, his secrets, his insight, his clout.

Not so Shandi.

She wanted his body, the pleasure he could give her. She took it with enthusiasm. She gave him back the same. She wasn't shy, and he doubted she understood what it meant to be inhibited.

If he'd thought her a breath of fresh air earlier, now he was blown away.

They'd made it from the library back to the elevator without being seen, adjusting what clothing they'd missed the first time they'd laughingly pulled themselves together before the doors opened onto the sixteenth floor. Not that the state of their dress or undress mattered.

No one who saw them gave them a second look. It was the nature of Hush not to stare. It was also the nature of Hush to provide amenities beyond complimentary brandy. In the bathroom, next to the vanity jars of cotton balls and Q-tips, he'd found one containing condoms.

Once he'd locked the door behind them, turned off his cell phone, unplugged the room's land line from the connection on the wall, opened the balcony doors and let in the night sky she told him she loved…after all of that, he undressed her.

He stood her at the foot of his bed, placed a silencing finger to her lips and bent to slip her feet out of her shoes and socks. Her toenails were painted to match the mask on her face. An iridescent blue-green that reminded him of a mermaid's tail.

He lifted her foot, kissed her arch, her ankle, the curve of her calf, finding himself moments later nuzzling her knees and inhaling the scent of sex. He hardened immediately, dropped his forehead to her belly and groaned. "I can't believe what you do to me."

"It's the outfit," she teased. "Takes you back to being a schoolboy."

If only that wasn't the humiliating truth. Not the outfit but the fact that he'd lost anything that resembled control, that he had no more finesse than a randy teen. And that he wasn't sure he cared.

Sex hadn't been this mind-blowing, this spontaneous, this much fun in more years than he wanted to remember. He kissed her thighs there beneath the hem of her skirt while he eased down the zipper.

"Speaking of you as a schoolboy—"

"Which I was trying *not* to do," he interrupted to add.

Laughing, she shimmied out of the skirt; it pooled around her ankles and she kicked it away. "You never did tell me that story."

"What story?" He responded without thinking. At the first sight of her panties all twisted and damp and revealing, his blood had rushed from his brain to his cock.

"The one all about Quentin Marks."

He stood, went to work on the buttons of her blouse. "No story there. I told you. Boring years of a lot of work and very little sleep."

"Is that why you're going back to Austin? To catch up on your sleep?" she asked as he pushed her sleeves down her arms, trapping her in the fabric at her elbows.

He thought of her bound and at his mercy, and got harder. He turned her, twisted the shirt's dangling tails into a cloth rope and tied her wrists together at the small of her back. Then he pulled off her panties and stood back to observe his handiwork.

He stared at her beautifully rounded and naked ass, her legs he wanted to feel wrapped around him. When she turned back to face him, he took in the thrust of her breasts, the tips that were pink and pebbled and matched the bare lips of her pussy beneath the narrow strip of hair left above.

"I guess what they say is true," she said, the comment finally bringing his gaze up to meet hers. "That men can only use one head at a time. Since you seem to have forgotten I asked you a question."

He couldn't even think of what she'd said when the way she looked, naked and hindered and his, consumed him. "Remind me. I've got a one-track mind at the moment."

She didn't answer right away. Instead she strummed him with her gaze until he vibrated under her attention, until it itched unbearably to be wearing his clothes. He kicked off his shoes and pulled his shirt over his head, losing several buttons in the process.

He went to work next on his belt and pants, skinning them off until he wore only the second skin of his boxers and his socks—the latter of which he lost at the questioning lift of her brow. He would have peeled off the former had he not needed to feel that he hadn't lost all his control.

And then he stood there, feeling like the one held captive when she was the one all tied up. The past two evenings he'd spent sitting at the bar, he'd fantasized about having her naked beneath him. He'd just never expected the anticipation to knot him up this fiercely.

"About that question," she finally said, her lashes fluttering down as she closed her eyes briefly and took a deep breath. "Why don't I remind you later?"

When had a woman ever looked at him the way Shandi did? Or had he been too wrapped up in his own world to have seen? No. Of that much he was certain. She was a new experience when he thought he'd seen it all.

Hands at his hips, he swallowed once before he was able to speak. "Later works for me."

She tugged playfully at her bonds, her smile an enticing combination of dimples and mischief. "I mean, I've never been a bondage kind of girl. And I think I'm liking it.

Her voice, her words…he took both as an invitation and approached, dropping to his knees at her feet. When he slid his palms from her knees up her thighs, she sucked in a quick breath and exhaled slowly, her legs trembling.

Smiling to himself, he kissed her belly. Her skin was softly scented and smooth, cooled by the room's air. He warmed her with his mouth and made his way lower, leaving a trail of tiny bite marks to remind her of where he'd been. She giggled and whimpered; the sounds were nervous echoes of his own impatience.

And when he finally settled his lips over the sweet bud of her clit, used his thumbs to spread open her folds and slipped his tongue inside her, he wasn't sure which of their sighs was the louder.

She took a step back, made contact with the bed and sat, pulling her heels to hips. She said nothing, simply urged him closer with the bold lift of one brow and the bolder way she parted her knees.

He couldn't resist and bent to taste her, sipping at her moisture and loving how ready she already was, how salty-sweet, how tart. He sucked her into his mouth and eased a finger inside.

She clenched around him, lifted her hips, and suddenly he didn't want her bound at all. He wanted her hands in his hair, her fingers wrapped around his cock, her palms massaging the pressure points of his pecs.

"Sit up," he said, getting to his feet and helping her up with a hand wrapped around her upper arm.

"I hope you don't think you're done," she teased, turning when he urged her around.

"I'm done with not having you touch me." He finished with the knots around her wrists, pulled the blouse off and tossed it on top of the pile of his own discarded clothes.

She stayed where she was, reaching back with one hand to find his erection and hold him. He tightened in her hand, pulsed and throbbed and wondered if he'd ever be able to take his time with this woman. Nothing but the simplest contact and he was ready to go off.

Turning then to face him, she lifted him free of his boxers, sinking to her knees and taking him into her mouth. She ringed her fingers around the base of his shaft and squeezed. Blood pumped at the constriction, engorging him fully.

He watched as she wrapped her lips around the head of his cock, as she swirled her tongue over the hard ridge and the seam beneath. He couldn't even breathe for the longest time, caught between the visual candy of her mouth, her tits, her heart-shaped ass and the sensations rocking through him.

"Enough," he finally growled, helping her to her feet. She pressed her body to his. "You're making me crazy."

"In a good way, I hope," she mumbled, her mouth busy with his chest, her lips tugging his hair, her tongue circling one nipple before moving to the other.

He couldn't think about anything but taking her. "Now that you're naked, I have all these things I want to do. But the only one that matters is being inside you."

"Then what in the world are you waiting for?" she asked and slipped a hand between them to rub the bead of moisture he'd released.

Hands at her waist, he held her, swiveled and took her with him as he fell back to the bed. They landed with legs and arms tangled, her knee on top of his thigh, her shoulder in the crook of his elbow. Their chests rose and fell until, laughing, Shandi scrambled on top.

The first thing he did was take down her hair. The

long blond strands fell like rainwater, washing down her back and spilling forward onto his chest. So soft and sweetly scented, as if they'd fallen from the sky. He wrapped a lock around his fingers and used it like a rope to tug her down.

Her mouth was already open when she found his and eased her tongue inside. He cupped a palm to the back of her head and held her, kissing her while he reached for a condom, then for his cock to guide himself between her legs. She lifted her body and settled over him, sliding down the full length of his shaft until their bodies were flush.

She stopped. He groaned, pulsing inside of her as she held him in her warmth. When she began to move, she moved slowly, rotating her hips and grinding against him, raising up, coming down, repeating each step and setting a rhythm he couldn't help but meet.

He pushed into her, pulled out, tore his mouth from hers to breathe against her neck where her skin was hot and damp. The buildup rose to a frantic, fevered pitch; bracing her hands on his shoulders, she sat up, closed her eyes and tossed back her hair for the ride.

The biggest mistake he could have made was to watch her, but that's what he did. He watched her eyes screw shut. He watched her lips part and her tongue catch the edge of her teeth. He watched the thrust of her breasts, the pebbled tips harden, the flex of her abs.

It was when he glanced down to where her sex was spread open by his that he lost it. Seeing her beautifully pale skin, the pink flesh of her sex and all of it rubbing his dark hair and swallowing his cock was the straw on his camel's very weak and very loaded back.

The moment he surged upward, she squeezed, crying out and coming around him. Her shuddering spasms vibrated through him. He dug his fingers into her thighs and let go. His release shook him, a powerful burst that left him drained.

She collapsed against him, and he rolled them both to their sides, their bodies still joined. A long time passed before the remnants of their tremors evanesced.

And he lay there for several more minutes, wondering why this woman had come into his life now when he was building his future so very far away.

"I LIKE YOUR FACE," QUENTIN said once Shandi had climbed back into bed beside him after scrubbing away the paint. "The makeup was amazing, but it's nice to see who I'm making love with."

For some reason, the "making love" tag applied to what they'd done made her uncomfortable. Putting sex with Quentin into those terms gave the act an emotional weight with which she didn't want to be burdened.

What they were sharing was fun, and she was looking forward to the week ahead. But she was also realistic and knew that once he'd finished the meetings for which he was here, that was it. They were done. *Fini. Hasta la vista,* baby.

Propped on one elbow, she cuddled up to his side. "You shouldn't have to see me to know who I am."

"Hmm." He pillowed his head on one wrist and frowned. "Who are you?"

"I'm the woman trying to find out who *you* are. You are hardly very forthcoming, sir."

"*Sir.* I like that. Say it again."

She looped a lock of his hair around her fingers. "Wrong. This is *my* fantasy. I'm the lowly student bartender in bed with a rock and roll legend."

He turned his head toward her, his gaze a harsh scowl. "There is nothing about you that is lowly. And trust me, being a legend is not all it's cracked up to be."

See, *this* was what she wanted to know. How he felt about who he was. How he felt about her in that context. It would explain so much about why she was the one here with him. "Then it's the legend thing that's driving you back to Texas."

"I'm not being driven. I'm going back to Texas because I've been away too long." He shifted to stare at the ceiling and captured her hand against him where now she was toying with the hair on his chest. "I need grounding. I'm starting to believe my own hype and I don't like it."

Interesting that he would judge himself that way, by the opinions of others. Or that he'd have made it as far as he had and still not feel he was grounded. "I've heard a lot of the hype. And other than the paternity-suit thing—" at the mention of that, he groaned "—none of it has been negative."

"Even the cynical-bastard part?" he asked, his heart beating harder beneath her hand than it had been.

"I'm pretty sure those were your words." She paused

and, when he didn't respond right away, pressed on. "But it does make me curious."

"About?" he asked, the single-word remark hardly encouraging.

Not that she let that stop her. "Whether it's believing your own hype that's making you that way. Or whether it's all the other things you've seen."

"Call it a combination," he said, dropping the obviously uncomfortable subject again.

She picked it right back up. "How so?"

At that, he closed his eyes, shook his head, turned from his back to his side to face her. When he looked at her again, she knew he was done talking. "If you let go of that bone, I swear I'll give you another."

She rolled her eyes and punched him in the shoulder before scooting up to sit at the head of the bed. "I've had enough of your bone for one night, mister. I'm not even sure I'll be able to walk out of here."

He reached for the ends of her hair, swirled them over her nipple as he would a paintbrush. "You can spend the night, you know."

"I can't. I need to sleep. I've got class in the morning and I'm having lunch with two girlfriends before work." The look in his eyes—desire, disappointment, determination—was almost enough to make her give in.

It was a powerful emotion, this lust they shared, and she wished they had the time to explore where it might lead. "If I stay, I won't be good for anything tomorrow."

"Hmm," was the only sound he made.

"What's that supposed to mean?"

"I'm trying to decide if I'm more impressed by your priorities or by the wet spot you make."

"Argh! Men!" She swung her legs around and hopped from the bed, searching for her clothes. "And you wonder why you can't get a girl to stick around."

He laughed, stacking pillows behind him as he sat to watch her dress. "I could ring room service and have a Mrs. Cyprus or two delivered."

"Don't you dare," she said, zipping her skirt over her panties. "You want to stop believing your own hype? You can start right there. No one likes a show-off."

His mouth twisted wryly while the twinkle in his eyes was pure fun. "And here I thought you were jealous."

"Oh, I am. But I'm not naive, nor am I stupid." She frowned as she fought her blouse's buttons. "I don't want to think about the women you'll have after me any more than I want to acknowledge the ones who came before."

When she looked back up, she found his gaze on her, his regard intense in a way that brought to mind his earlier statement about making love.

Her fingers shook as she propped a foot on the end of the bed and pulled on her sock. "Whatever you're thinking, stop it already."

He shifted higher in the bed, the sheet across his lap dipping dangerously low. "What time do you get off work tomorrow night?"

She finished with her second sock and slipped into her shoes. "I'm scheduled until two. Why?"

"Spend the night with me tomorrow."

Eyes closed, she breathed deeply. "I can't. Thursday's just as crazy as tomorrow."

"Thursday night then. Take it off."

"I can't afford to miss a night of tips. Too many bills to pay." Why was he insisting? And why in the world was she turning him down when this is what she'd been wanting since the first night they'd met?

She did what she could to finger-comb her hair and pull it into a French braid. "But that doesn't mean you can't stop by and watch me work."

His gaze grew heavy lidded. His nostrils flared. Beneath the sheet, he pulled up one knee, and she didn't have to wonder why. "If I do, are you going to wear a skirt so I can enjoy your legs?"

And on that note she headed for the door. "You keep that up and you'll never see my legs again."

"Don't make promises you can't keep, Shandi." When she glanced back, he was sitting with his hands laced behind his head, the king of all he surveyed. "I might be a cynical bastard, but I can still tell the difference between a woman who's faking it and one who's having a good time."

"Then you shouldn't have any trouble figuring out that I'm not pulling your leg. First, second *or* that very impressive third," she said, opening the door and walking down the hallway to the fading sound of his laughter.

6

FOUND IN BOTTOM OF POOL:
One pink, diamond-studded collar.
Does NOT belong to Eartha Kitty!
V.V. important to locate owner.
Look for man with matching leash!!!
(snicker)

ON HER WAY OUT OF THE hotel Shandi glanced toward the bar out of habit—only instead of her focus taking in Armand working the thinning crowd, she found herself caught by the unusual sight of Evan Harcourt drinking.

Unusual because he couldn't afford Erotique unless she was there to comp his drinks.

Having washed away the smears of mask she hadn't left on Quentin's pillows, she didn't feel too weird about being seen. Her outfit wasn't any more outrageous than what was worn by a lot of bar patrons on the make—even if her blouse was a wrinkled disaster.

She climbed up onto the stool next to Evan. "Are you lost, little boy?"

He'd been staring down into his beer, a shock of dark hair obscuring his eyes, and he didn't even move except to shift his gaze toward her. "Since when do you spend your night off where you work? Oh, wait. Banana man's staying here, isn't he?"

"Me being here isn't the issue," she said, changing the subject. "Why are *you* here? I figured with April gone you'd be out with the guys."

"You figured wrong," he mumbled. "I figured wrong."

Uh-oh. "What did you figure wrong? How long have you been here? And, while I'm in interrogation mode, who's been paying for your drinks?"

"You're going to." He chuckled. Chuckled again because he obviously thought he was funny. "I'm running up a tab in your name."

"Gee, thanks." His beer was almost empty. She reached for the mug and swallowed half of what was left. "Here, drink up and we'll go home."

"I hung up on April."

Shandi frowned. "What? When?"

"Earlier. At home." He threaded his fingers through the handle and palmed his mug. "I called her to see if she could get back tonight."

"And she told you no," Shandi said and sighed.

He shrugged. "That wasn't why I hung up on her."

She didn't figure it was. He should've been used to April telling him no by now. "Then why did you?"

"Because she got bent out of shape about me critcizing her *Daddy*," he said and downed the rest of the beer.

'Nuff said, Shandi mused, crossing her legs as she sat back against the bar chair's inverted-triangular back. "Evan, how many times are we going to have this conversation? You either deal with April's family or you don't."

"Right." He wavered, caught himself before falling into her lap. "Deal with them when I don't even know them."

"I hope you're not blaming April for that?"

He collapsed back, pushed his dark hair from his face with both hands, didn't say a word.

And so she did. "You know, there's nothing stopping you from going to Connecticut and introducing yourself."

"Tonight?" he asked, glancing over at her with bleary eyes.

"Uh, no." Shandi didn't even want to imagine April's reaction should Evan show up wasted at four in the morning. "Tonight you're coming home with me and going to bed."

"Bed, huh? What about banana man?"

She signaled to Armand for a pen to sign her tab. "Not to bed with me. I'll sleep in mine. You'll sleep in yours. Like always. We can talk about your trip over breakfast."

"We don't eat breakfast."

And he sure as hell wasn't going to be wanting to put anything in his stomach come morning. "That's okay. I seriously doubt you'll remember this conversation ten minutes from now."

He swiveled his chair to the side, stared across the dimly lighted bar where clusters of patrons sat at the glossy black tables, seeming to finally focus on the Tamara de Lempicka painting hanging on the back wall. "I've wished so many times that April was more like you."

She had to be careful here, her loyalties divided between her two best friends. "If she was, then she wouldn't be the woman you fell in love with."

"No, but she'd be independent. She'd be on her own." His voice was clear and sober, his expression strangely the same. "Our relationship would be about us, not this twisted threesome that I can't deal with."

She'd never seen Evan this down before. She'd seen him drunk, sure, but never wallowing in his misery. And for the first time she found herself really and truly scared by what he was saying.

Scared because she didn't know what April would do without him, what Evan would do without her.

That thought caused Shandi to think of Quentin and all his women, Evan with his one and to know that this was what she wanted—a man who felt so much for her that not having her was more than he could bear.

She wondered if Quentin had ever felt that way about a woman. Or if the cynical beast didn't believe in love. Not that what he believed mattered—and why was she even *thinking* about the word *love?* This fling might be the best time she'd ever had, but it wasn't going anywhere.

The distance between New York and Austin was way

too far. The distance between the life she wanted and Round-Up even further. Getting to her feet, she groaned, feeling all her sore and aching body parts, then schooled her face into a smile.

"C'mon, lover boy," she said, grabbing Evan by the biceps and steadying him as he climbed down to join her. "Let's get you home."

"Home. Right." He stopped as if he'd decided not to leave and suddenly sobered. "The place where I live platonically with you instead of with the woman I love."

"So kick me out and invite her in." She experienced a small flash of panic. She couldn't afford to live on her own and would have to hurriedly rustle up a roommate if Evan gave her the boot.

"I do that, all three of us will be looking for a cardboard box. My grandmother's not a word mincer," he said with a bit of a slur, frowning briefly at the expression. "If April's living at the apartment, I'm a goner."

"Well, we'll figure it out." Shandi wrapped an arm around Evan's waist and made for the door. "We're just not going to be doing it until you've had eight hours, a handful of aspirin and a gallon or two of java."

Shandi—*Must* schedule Saturday's makeup session.
The fund-raiser's at 8:00.
I need to be there at 5:00.
Can you do me at 2:00?
Kisses, Kit

WHEN SHANDI MET APRIL FOR lunch on Wednesday, it wasn't at Amuse Bouche after all. Kit Prescott, Hush's PR director and the best girlfriend Shandi had made at the hotel, joined them at Aquavit.

April had come home from Connecticut with what her father considered an allowance, what the rest of the free world considered a month's income. She'd picked the restaurant because she was paying.

Shandi sat across the table from the other two. It gave her time to study the contrast of Kit's blond hair with April's brunette. Kit's blue eyes with April's that were the green of new spring. Kit's unconventionally wild beauty with the delicate breeding of April's blue blood.

"You two have no idea how great you're going to look when I get this print ad's mock-up put together for class," Shandi said with a sigh, wishing she could find the last missing piece to her ad's puzzle. It was a marketing campaign for hair color, and her girlfriends had agreed to model.

Still, she knew she needed something more, something…bigger. She'd just yet to pin it down. "Are we still on for Sunday's photo shoot? I'll buy lunch—or at least have Chef send it downstairs." She'd managed, with Kit's help, to arrange to use Exhibit A. "It'll be fun."

Kit nodded, tucking back her hair and exposing chic sapphire studs. "As long as I survive Saturday night in one piece. I have *no* idea how I got talked into working on the committee for this fund-raiser. I mean, seriously.

Do we really need to save an art gallery when the AIDS epidemic in Africa is taking so many innocent lives?"

"Not to diminish that particular tragedy at all," April said, reaching for her wineglass, her nails shimmering with a soft copper sheen that matched her silk shift and her eye shadow. "But you do realize you're talking to two art students, don't you? One who is planning to eventually open a gallery to showcase her own jewelry designs?"

"Of course I didn't mean that as a slight to either of you," Kit said with a wide-eyed gasp. She pressed a hand to her chest, toyed with a dainty platinum chain. "Shandi, please tell me you know that."

Her simple lemon tank dress accessorized by nothing but a kiwi-and-melon-colored scarf, her nails not accessorized at all, Shandi grinned. "I know that. And April knows that. She's just giving you a hard time because that's what she's good at doing lately."

"And what's that supposed to mean?" April asked, her brow arched as she returned her wineglass to the table. Sitting back, she folded her hands in her lap. "Is that some sort of dig at my fight with Evan?"

Kit glanced from one woman to the other, reached for her Kate Spade clutch and scooted back her chair. "Excuse me, will you both? I need to visit the ladies' room."

Smoothing the tablecloth next to her empty plate, Shandi waited until Kit was out of earshot before she pounced the way she'd been waiting to do since hauling a drunk Evan Harcourt out of Erotique the night before.

"I'm not going to get in the middle of it." She dropped her voice to a pleading whisper. "C'mon, April. That's not fair to any of us."

April looked down and away, rubbing the pad of her index finger over the base of her wineglass. "He called me last night. We were in the middle of dinner, and he called and asked if I could come home."

"So?" Shandi lifted her glass of water and took a sip. "I'd love to have a man who wanted to be with me badly enough that he'd do that."

"You don't understand. Neither of you understand." April dramatically swept her hair back over her shoulders. "You don't have the sort of family obligations I have."

That was such bull Shandi wanted to plug up her nose. But she was a better friend than that. "Okay, then, explain them to me. What obligations keep you tied to Connecticut?"

April's frown signaled true confusion, a youthful confusion, causing Shandi to suddenly feel so very old. "Everything, what do you mean?"

"Spell it out for me. What can't you give up?" She turned her chair sideways and rested against the wall. "Dinner when your father is struck by a whim? Shopping with your mother? Walking the family dog?"

April glared. "That's not funny."

"Neither is me having to drag your boyfriend's wasted ass out of Erotique at 1:00 a.m." Shandi leaned forward, keeping her voice low. "I barely got him out of the taxi and up the stairs before he passed out. He was gone when I got up for class, but I know he slept on the sofa."

"At least he slept," April admitted softly. "I didn't. I couldn't. I kept hearing that disconnect sound from his phone beeping in my ear."

"Sweetie, you've got to talk to him about this. It's not going to go away. He feels left out, and I can't say I blame him."

"So you blame me," April said and tightened her gaze until Shandi felt the guilty pinch.

"No." She shook her head. "It's not my place to blame anyone. It's not my relationship. You're both my friends, and I don't want either of you to get hurt. Thing is, the way this is going, if you two don't talk, it's going to happen."

April's eyes reddened but didn't water. "I don't know how to make a choice like this. Between Evan and my family? How can I do that?"

This is what Shandi didn't get. What she'd never get. She toyed with the hem of the tablecloth draped in her lap. "Why does it have to be a choice? Why can't you just include Evan in your family?"

"It's not that simple," April said, shaking her head.

"It is if you want it to be," Shandi replied, because to her it couldn't be more so.

Then again, her blood wasn't as blue as April's—though the Fosseys of Round-Up were just as rigid in their expectations as the Carters of Connecticut seemed to be.

Maybe April wasn't ready to make the same self-interested break from her past as Shandi had. And honestly? She wouldn't blame her friend. Not everyone shared her own consuming drive.

April huffed. "Tell Trevor that it's simple. He brought Stefan Navarro to dinner." She gave an affected roll of her eyes. "Or he tried. Daddy wasn't having any of it."

"So who won?"

"You say that like we're at war," April said, her gaze growing narrow.

Shandi simply shrugged. "If not a war, then at least a battle."

"You don't even talk to your family," April snapped, tossing her napkin from her lap onto the table. "Why do you think you know so much about mine?"

"I don't. But I do know you and I do know Evan." Shandi paused, letting that sink in. "I also know that making a choice or a stand isn't easy. I did it. It was either stay in Round-Up and live the life my family had chosen for me or come here and live my own."

"It's not the same," April said, weakening.

"So says you," Shandi responded, feeling even more a wise old crone in the making. But seeing her girlfriend's dilemma made it easier to cement the decisions she'd made to get out on her own.

April offered a wry grin. "Yeah. I do. And thanks. You're a good friend."

Shandi chuckled as Kit rejoined them. "Man, the things we put ourselves through for love and money."

"Tell me about it," Kit practically huffed, settling into

the conversation as if she'd never left. "And this fundraiser isn't even *my* money. Not to mention it's all volunteer. I'm not getting a thing out of it."

"Besides an awesome makeover, you mean?" Shandi reminded her.

"That, yes. And then there's the good karma." She waggled both brows. "Not to mention that I'm being escorted by the gallery owner's son, who could easily be Orlando Bloom's older and way sexier brother."

Shandi pictured Orlando Bloom, quickly replaced him with Quentin, pictured Quentin standing between Kit and April and looking down, his ivory linen jacket hanging open, his skin bronzed, his eyes and hair all scotch and honey, a big golden cat on the prowl.

And that was it. Exactly what her ad campaign needed. Quentin was Kit's blonde and April's brunette combined. The tawny hybrid. The perfect blend of two palettes. She laughed to herself. "I can't believe it."

"What can't you believe?" April asked.

Shandi shook her head, no longer hearing the buzz of conversation in the restaurant. "I have been racking my brain to come up with the angle I need for this class project."

"You don't need us anymore?" Kit asked.

"Oh, yes. You're both on the hook." She wasn't about to let either of them off. "You're both perfect for what I want to do. But I needed one more thing, and Kit's Orlando Bloom comment triggered it."

Would he do it if she asked? A Grammy-winning record producer stooping to help out a poor college kid? She laughed aloud at that. At the idea of Quentin stooping to do anything. But for her he might just pitch in.

All she had to do was make sure he understood she didn't want to use *that* Quentin Marks—the one the world thought him to be. She wanted the man she knew. An anonymous symbol, the sexy epitome of what women looked for in a man.

"You're going to use Orlando Bloom in your ad?" April asked, reaching for the thin strap of her purse on the back of her chair and counting out the cash to pay the bill.

"No," Shandi replied. "Even better."

Kit lifted a brow. "Better than Orlando Bloom? Now that I've got to see."

"Oh, you will." Shandi got to her feet, grabbed up her wallet, already eager to get Quentin to agree. "But you're going to have to wait until Sunday."

"IF YOU'RE NOT BUSY, HOW would you feel about helping me out this weekend? I've got a class project I'm working on, and with your input I think I can ace it," Shandi said to Quentin Wednesday night.

The question came moments after he'd climbed onto the stool he'd claimed as his own at the far end of the bar and before he'd had a chance to tell her that she looked so good in those tight black tuxedo pants that getting her out of them had become his official fantasy.

She didn't mention a word about Tuesday night in the library or the wee hours of Wednesday morning in his bed. She hadn't said a word about how he'd put her off when she'd quizzed him about the state of his mind. Or about the way he hadn't wanted to talk about himself at all.

All she'd done was grab a glass, pour his drink and smile at him as if she knew all of his secrets. It was enough to make a man go mad. To make him admit that it was useless to avoid a woman's need to know, a lost cause to hide.

Even though he wasn't talking, he liked it that Shandi was interested. "I knew it. You're just like all the rest. Wanting me for all the ways I can help your career," he teased.

She grinned, buzzed her lips and tongue in a raspberry, waved over his head at someone he didn't turn to see. "It took you all this time to figure that out?"

Cheeky wench. He didn't even know what to say to her amusing confession. "What sort of project?"

She hesitated, an empty drink shaker in one hand, a towel in the other, her head tilted to one side as she considered him. "You know what? I think I'll wait and tell you about it later."

He lifted his drink, studied her over the rim of the glass. "Why not tell me about it now?"

"Because I'm working and because *you've* had another long day of meetings. I can see it in your face." She gestured toward him with the shaker. "You need to relax, take advantage of your bartender's friendly ear."

He shrugged. He was prepared. He wasn't going to fall prey to her plentiful charms. But he did like the way she noticed his mood. The way she was more interested in hearing about his day than filling him in on her plans.

He swirled the melting ice in his glass. "I'll worm it out of you sooner or later, you know."

"I have no doubt. You do have your sneaky ways of getting to me," she said, adding a wink. "But I should've waited to bring it up. I am way too busy tonight to get into the details anyway."

"Busy, huh?" He swiveled his chair to glance around the near-empty room before glancing back at her. "Uh, yeah. I see that."

She stuck out her tongue, leaving him alone while she checked with the rest of the bar's patrons. He watched as she walked away, took in the length of her legs she'd yet to wrap around him. He'd had them tangled with his, bracketing his, warm and smooth as they'd rubbed against his.

What he wanted was to feel her heels digging hard and pulling him in. What he needed was to get his mind off bedding her or else he was going to be walking out of here with a baseball-bat-worthy wood.

Getting hard wasn't the issue. The issue was that he couldn't think of anything else when she was around. She consumed him, enchanted him.

He wanted more, wanted all of her, was certain that he'd never get enough.

A part of him wondered if she was truly as special as she appeared to be. Or if he was so desperate to be free of his cynicism that he was seeing what he wanted to see instead of what was there.

If he was indulging in this fantasy because he didn't like the reality of his personal life. If he was looking for more ways than moving to Austin to bring about the change his sanity was demanding.

Once she'd finished drawing a beer for one customer, listening to another cry into his, she returned to where Quentin was waiting, wiping down the slick ebony surface where a third had left a sizable cash tip.

She tucked the bills into a snifter beneath the bar. "And that is why I'm standing here and you're sitting there. This is my bread and butter. You're just the cherry on top. So, now, tell me what went on today. Have you decided which lucky firm will be getting your business?"

Talking about cherries was dangerous conversation, but he was having hell tearing his mind away from the way she'd looked riding him. "I have, actually. The terms were all competitive, so it ended up being more about compatibility, vision and control."

"Yours, no doubt." When he nodded, she smiled, adding, "Good for you. I'm glad you got what you wanted."

"I usually do," he responded offhandedly. And then he winced. "Sorry. That was crass."

"Actually it was honest." She cleared his empty glass from the bar, added it to a tub of dirty glassware when he declined a refill. "Why apologize? I think your accomplishments have earned you a few rights."

He leaned closer, his forearms braced on the edge of the bar. "Not the right to give up thinking before I open my mouth."

"I don't know about that." She reached for her own bottle of water, unscrewed the cap and drank. "You obviously think too much since it's hell prying anything good out of you."

Tenacious. Focused. A dog with a bone. "That's because there's nothing to pry. I told you. I went from high school band to college band. Every day of my life since has been about music."

"No." Her tone dropped. She held the spout of the bottle in front of her lips. "You didn't tell me. At least, not until now."

"And see? It's nothing." He shrugged off the truth instead of letting her dig.

He didn't want her to discover there wasn't a damn thing to find beyond what she saw on the surface. He'd been on the same single-minded career track all of his life, and that was it. Who he was. What he was.

He was proud of all he'd accomplished, but he'd given up too much along the way. Going back to Austin was the first step in correcting that. In reclaiming the rest of his life from the public. He was starting over, and it felt so damn good that he smiled.

"I'm not buying it," she finally said, screwing the cap back on the bottle and storing it away. "It's not nothing. It's huge. It's outstanding. You're only—what?—thirty-five? Thirty-seven? And you've done so much."

He stared at her for a very long time, at the blue of her eyes that shimmered, at her smile that seemed to be a part of her soul.

Her adoration wasn't that of a young fan who thought he could do no wrong. It wasn't that of an aspiring musician seeking a word.

It was that of a woman interested in a man. And it hit him like a punch to the gut. "Do you have a break soon?"

She arched the long column of her neck as she studied the bar's clock. He had to look away, to look down. Emotions rolled through him, untried and uncomfortable, sharp blades of an unfamiliar need.

"Actually yes. I can take one now."

He didn't respond. He was already headed for the door she'd pointed out yesterday. The one that opened from Erotique into the bar's back room.

7

SHE MET HIM JUST INSIDE the doorway. He backed her into the wall, pinned her wrists over her head with one hand, stared down into her eyes. "Do you know how much I want you?"

Her gaze crawled from his chest that heaved like a bellows up to his nostrils that flared. She pulled in a deep breath, blew it out slowly. "I have a pretty good idea."

"God, Shandi." He closed his eyes, opened them only after he'd gotten one last grasp on his control. "You're the only woman who's ever done this to me. You make me forget everything but being with you."

"I do?" she whispered, her words barely audible.

He didn't answer. He bent to nuzzle her neck, to kiss the hollow of her throat, the soft indentation beneath her ear. He inhaled her. She was fresh and sweet and everything he wasn't, even while she was wiser than her years.

"Come back to my room."

She shook her head. "I can't," she said, and he prayed she didn't mean *I won't*. "I only have fifteen minutes. We'd barely get the door locked by then."

"I'm not leaving," he growled into her hair.

"I didn't say you had to."

He raised his head; his gaze bored into hers. "Where?"

She pressed her lips together, glanced over his right shoulder, over his left, took him by the hand and ordered him to, "C'mon."

He followed. She wound her way behind cases of beer, boxes of liquor and shelves of supplies—stir sticks, napkins, olives, peanuts, grenadine, mixers and salt.

The corner was dark, but he saw the sign for the employee restroom and urged her to hurry. The minute they were both inside, she closed the door behind him.

When she reached for the light, he stopped her, pulling her fingers to the front of his shirt. She chuckled softly under her breath, unbuttoning him as quickly as he struggled to unbutton her.

That done, she went to work unfastening his pants, sprinkling desperate kisses over the bare skin of his chest, her tongue circling a nipple, her teeth catching him there.

He groaned, loving the way she knew how to touch him, trembling when she did.

Her fingers found his cock, and she dropped to her knees, lifting him free of his boxers and taking him into her mouth. He leaned back against the door, his hands clenched into fists at his side.

The darkness intensified all that he was feeling—the moist warmth of her mouth, the cup of her tongue to his head, the tight ring of her fingers, the blood rushing to fill him until he thought he would burst.

He didn't want to come this way. He didn't want to

rush. He wanted time and space and knew he had neither. He reached for Shandi, pulled her to her feet, pushed his pants to his knees and helped her work hers down and off.

And then he bent to taste her, to make sure she was ready, that her anticipation was in sync with his. He lifted her by the hips once he had and backed her into the smooth tile wall. Her legs came around his waist. She dug her heels into the base of his spine.

Sheathed, he drove into her, gripping her bottom and holding on to her thighs as he thrust. He could smell her woodsy shampoo, the softly scented soap she'd used to bathe. He could smell her sex, a mix of grapefruit and the salty marine of the sea.

He ground the base of his shaft against her, rubbing, arousing, and it wasn't a minute later that he felt her first contractions. She cried out, her hands slapping against the tile as she came.

Her spasms did him in. His face buried in the crook of her neck, he followed, pulsing, pumping, spilling himself into her body there in the dark. He came down slowly from the high to which she'd taken him.

And then he realized what they'd done.

What he'd done.

They were in a bathroom in the back room of a bar. Talk about crass. What in the hell was wrong with him? He eased her down to stand on the floor. She groaned, and guilt seized him.

"I'm sorry." He rested his forehead against hers, gently kissed her eyelids and the bridge of her nose. "I don't know what I was thinking."

Her laugh cleared the room's murky shadows. "I'm pretty sure that was mostly about feeling. If we were supposed to be thinking, nobody told me."

She bent to retrieve her pants. He discarded the condom and repaired his clothes, as well, grumbling under his breath as he put himself back together. "I'm too old for this."

"For what?" she asked, reaching over and flipping on the light. He blinked. She blinked. The bulb sputtered. "To act on what you want? To go for it?"

Her expression was a cross between hurt and confusion. He didn't want her to feel either. "Not to show more restraint. Not to treat you better."

At that she laughed. "If you treated me any better, I'd need a wheelchair. Besides, I don't want you restrained. Do you know what you're doing for my ego?"

Her remark shouldn't have cut him the way it did. He'd heard it so often, he should have been immune. But hearing it from Shandi brought home the depth of this attraction, the strength of its roots.

He shook them off and said, "I'm glad I could stroke it for you."

Stepping in front of him, she reached up, took his face in her hands. "It's more than that. You're the best time I've had in my life, and I've only known you for a few days. What kind of sense am I supposed to make out of that? Of you, being who you are and wanting me?"

"Why shouldn't I want you?" He didn't understand her surprise at his attraction. "You're beautiful. You're open and honest and sexy as hell."

"I'm a bartender. A student." She let him go, backed toward the door. "You're world-famous and have traveled in circles that awe most of us mortals."

"Don't." He shoved his hands to his hips, hung his head, reined in his temper. "Don't put me on a pedestal. I'm human. A man. Nothing more."

She studied him with ardent curiosity. "Why do I get this feeling that you don't like yourself very much?"

"Because there are times that I don't," he answered, unnerved by her intuition.

"The hype thing, right?" she asked, and when he didn't respond, she wrapped him up in her arms and pressed her body to his. "Beating yourself up as much as you do has got to get old."

He couldn't help it. He chuckled. "I suppose."

"Remind me when I'm as successful as you not to be so hard on myself." Her fingertips kneaded their way down his spine. "I'd rather enjoy the pleasure of what I've earned than suffer all that needless pain."

He wanted to think her naive but knew that she wasn't. She was an optimist. A light in the dark. A go-getter who had the moxie not to fail—and not to fall if she did. "I don't think you have it in you to be hard on yourself."

At that she pushed him away, headed for the door with a self-deprecating laugh. "Remind me not to introduce you to any of my friends. They'll quickly set you straight."

"Oh, really," he said, his curiosity piqued.

"Yep. They'll consider it their duty to tell you every single detail of the truth," she replied, then just before walking out and back to work, added, "And I kind of like having my hype believed."

THREE-THIRTY THAT MORNING found Shandi sitting on the floor in her apartment in front of the windows, waiting for Evan and wishing she'd accepted Quentin's invitation to spend the night in his room. She still wasn't sure why she'd turned him down.

Physically she was certainly up for what a night in his bed offered; instead she was engaged in the routine of self-inflicted torture required to work the night's kinks from her body. She leaned forward and stretched, grabbing her toes and forcing her face to her knees.

When he'd told her he didn't think she had it in her to be hard on herself, she'd wanted to laugh. She was glad she hadn't, of course.

She liked him liking her, thinking she was more balanced, a better person, less insecure than she actually was. She'd been telling the truth when she'd said she liked having her own hype believed.

But now that she'd had time to think about it, his beating himself up did make more sense.

She didn't like that she couldn't get over where she'd come from. He didn't like that the life he'd lived, the dream he'd attained, had turned him into a cynical bastard.

She wondered what he'd expected to find at the end of the road. If he thought he'd be the same man who'd embarked on the trip once he reached his destination.

She picked up the phone on the floor at her side and dialed his room at Hush to ask him.

He answered on the second ring. "Quentin Marks."

She shivered at just hearing his voice and his name. "Did I wake you?"

"Hardly," he said gruffly. "I haven't slept much since meeting you."

Her stomach pitched. He made her nervous. So very nervous. It didn't make any sense how nervous she was.

"Well, that's not good. You need sleep so you'll have a clear head for all that big-dollar business you're doing."

"No. I need you. In my bed. Now."

Eyes closed, she inhaled a shaky breath. "You just had me."

"That was hours ago. Up against a wall. It wasn't enough."

He sounded angry; she didn't know if it was with her or with himself. "Quentin, what's going on?"

"Where?" he asked too casually for her to buy.

"Here. With us."

"We're having an affair."

She waited a long moment, listened to him breathe, listened to the silence swirling in the room. She could almost hear his heartbeat. Almost, because hers was too loud.

"An affair. Is that all?"

"No," he said, biting off the word and adding a litany of raw ones that spoke volumes about where his head was. "That's not all."

She had to be honest. "I think it's too much too soon."

"Yeah. I've been thinking the same."

His agreement didn't stop her from asking, "Do you want to come over for dinner tomorrow night?"

"What time?"

"Eight?"

"Are you cooking?"

"Yes."

"Forget the food. I'll have you."

Smiling, she got to her feet, walked barefoot toward the window, resting her forehead against the cool glass. "My roommate and his girlfriend will be here, too."

"Uninvite them."

"I can't," she said, nearly breathless. "I need them here."

"Why?"

"For protection."

"From me?"

"Yes."

Several long seconds ticked by before he quietly asked, "Do I frighten you?"

"No." An admission more telling than the first. "I frighten myself."

His laugh echoed with his own desperate need to understand. "You frighten me, too."

"I don't get it. Any of it."

"Neither do I."

She heaved a heavy sigh. Nothing ventured, nothing gained. Nothing to look back on and regret when she was eighty years old. "Then you'll come to dinner tomorrow."

"On one condition."

"What?"

"That you tell me about the class project you want me to help you ace."

APRIL SAT IN FRONT OF HER bedroom's vanity at four in the morning, unable to sleep and staring at her reflection in the oval mirror.

Staring, too, at the images of the room behind her—or what she could see by the soft light of her bedside lamp—a room furnished with antiques and original oil paintings.

Her mother's decorator's idea. Her father's checkbook.

She didn't know a single one of her classmates who had a dorm, apartment or loft to match what her parents had provided for her. Because of the way that made her feel self-conscious, she rarely entertained. Evan and Shandi were the only ones who spent time at her place.

She would never deny that she was spoiled. As Lawrence Elton Carter's little girl, she'd been that way from birth. What she hadn't realized was how it would feel to be the exception rather than the rule once she moved to the city and was living on her own.

Growing up, she'd been used to her girlfriends having similarly adorned bedrooms. Oh, sure, they'd hung posters of their favorite boy bands. She'd been all about Justin Timberlake and Nick Lachey.

But the posters had been easily hidden behind fabric wall hangings during her mother's garden club's Christmas Parade of Homes.

She'd hated that, strangers traipsing in and out, having her personal space open to the public—the sort of personal space even now she was missing.

She sighed, realizing that as beautiful as her room was, it wasn't her. She wanted what Shandi had, a bedroom of fun thrift-store finds.

Cushy pillows piled against a headboard fashioned like a theater marquee. A dressing screen in a Mae West print, an armoire that had once housed a popcorn machine, a clothes rack with stage hooks.

April wanted her home to be about her tastes, her interests, not decorated to reflect the Carter family's affluence.

But what she wanted most was Evan in her bed.

Instead he was sleeping on the sofa again. Her mother would be appalled—though not as much by Evan being there as by anyone doing more than sitting on that particular piece of furniture. It had been custom-covered in soft blues and greens to match the apartment's water lilies theme.

She didn't know why they weren't having sex. Well, no, that wasn't quite true. What she'd told Shandi was exactly how it was.

April had seen too many of her girlfriends sleep with guys who'd then proceeded to dump them. She didn't want to mess things up with Evan that way. To make love, then have him move on to another challenging conquest.

And, yes, she realized thinking that way didn't say much about her commitment to him or what they shared. But if she lost him for any reason, she wouldn't be able to stand it. She'd be miserable and then she'd be embarrassed when her daddy tried to buy him back.

Because that's exactly what would happen. Her daddy always said he hadn't met a man yet who couldn't be bought. Maybe it was time he met Evan.

Except Evan would never meet with her daddy's approval. He wasn't from the right family, didn't have the right blood running in his veins.

And that rejection would be so unfair because Evan Harcourt was the best man she'd ever known. He was kind and generous and caring. He made her laugh, and she couldn't stand not being with him.

She loved the way he gave her silly souvenirs from their dates; she had a drawer full of paper menus with the meals they'd eaten circled in red.

Subjecting him to her family seemed so wrong, even while refusing to include him was worse. God, but she was so confused—and suddenly so needed to hold Evan close.

She stood, tightened her knee-length silk wrapper at the waist and padded softly into the living room that was lit by only the moon coming through the bay window. "Evan? Are you asleep?"

He grumbled as he awakened, shifting up onto his elbows, then scooting up to sit in the corner of the sofa, rubbing at his eyes.

They'd cuddled up earlier and watched three episodes from the DVD of *Alias*'s first season. She was a total fanatic about that show.

"What's up?" He cleared his throat. "What's wrong?"

She curled up in the other corner, pulled her knees to her chest. "I wanted to talk."

"What time is it?" he asked, still groggy.

"Fourish."

"In the morning? What are you doing up?"

She shook her head. "I couldn't sleep. I missed you."

He stilled. "I've been right here all night."

"I know," she said with a sigh, making an admission she had often wondered if she would ever be brave enough to make. "But I wanted you with me."

"You wanted me with you how?" he asked, and she felt him tense.

"I don't like fighting with you. I don't like not talking about it when we fight. There's stuff going on here that we need to deal with." Shandi had been right. Getting out that much, acknowledging the existence of the problem, lifted a huge weight.

Evan was still rubbing sleep from his face. "And you want to deal with it at four in the morning?"

April shrugged because she didn't want to seem desperate. "I should let you sleep. It can wait."

"No. It can't. At least, I can't." Evan sighed, turned, dropped his feet to the floor and leaned forward as if he thought she'd come in to kick him out.

He spread his blanket over his lap, covering his legs that were bare but for his boxers. "I'm sorry for hanging up on you last night, the night before. Whenever it was."

She hated not being able to see him better. The room was too dark, his face in the shadows. And she cringed at the eggshells crackling between them. "I wouldn't have wanted to talk to me either. I was such a bitch."

He turned toward her then, stretched out a hand. "You weren't a bitch. I was being an ass. I wanted to see you. And I wasn't in the mood to wait."

She scooted closer and wrapped his fingers that were warm around hers that were freezing. "We need to do something about missing each other the way we do."

"Hey," he started, rubbing his free hand over her icy one, "I'm up for any suggestion that doesn't involve a change of address to an alley and a cardboard box."

She laughed because she'd considered that very same thing. "I was thinking of being proactive. You and me. Together. A team. And by *proactive* I don't mean getting drunk."

He hung his head. His hair fell over his brow. "Shandi told you, huh?"

"Yeah." Tucking her legs beneath her, April rested her cheek on his shoulder. "I don't like it when you do that, you know."

He nodded, rocking the both of them back and forth slowly. "So what did you have in mind?"

Here goes nothing, she mused, knowing it was everything she was risking. "I want us to move in together."

The rocking stopped. "What? How? My grandmother will kick me out on my ass if you're there. And your parents will do the same if I'm here."

"Then we get a place of our own. One no one in our families has any say in." She hurried on before he could interrupt. "I'll get a job, and we'll get Shandi to move with us. With three of us paying bills, we can do it."

He didn't answer right away. In fact, he was so silent for so long she began to worry that she'd said the wrong thing. That he didn't understand how very much she wanted to be with him.

And then he pulled his hands from hers, pushed back into the corner of the sofa, his withdrawal and the distance making her feel even worse.

Several long seconds ticked by before he spoke. "Why, April? Why now after so long of saying we need to be patient and not mess things up?"

But things were already messed up, weren't they? "You don't want to live together?"

"That's not what I said—"

"Then what?" she demanded, ignoring the tears aching to roll down her cheeks.

"I want to know if this is just so we'll see each other more often or if it's a permanent commitment?" His breathing was ragged, jerky, as if he couldn't get out what he wanted to say. "You and me as a couple for real?"

Did he think they weren't for real now? How could he when she'd just proposed sacrificing so much so they could be together…. And then it hit her. "You mean am I going to sleep with you?"

"That, too."

This was it then, wasn't it? The test of whether or not making love would bind them together forever or be the first brick to fall from the relationship they'd been meticulously building for months.

Were they ready? Were they strong enough? Or were they making the biggest mistake possible?

It was time to find out. Slowly, she unfolded her legs and got to her feet, holding out her hand and waiting breathlessly for him to take it.

8

Armand—I owe you BIG TIME for this!
I swear, the next shift you need me to cover, I'm
there! Oh, you might want to check the cocktail
napkins—I think we're down to one case.
Hugs, Shandi

BY THE TIME THURSDAY evening rolled around, Shandi
was a nervous wreck. She'd barely been able to keep
her mind on this morning's environmental-fragrancing
lecture for thinking of Quentin coming over tonight.

So silly to be that way.

It wasn't as if Quentin hadn't seen her naked…how
many times now? Still, this was different. She was baring
her passion, and it left her feeling vulnerable. He could
think her idea ridiculous. He could laugh at her dream.

But worst of all he could reject her. And that she
wouldn't be able to stand. Not when such a rejection
would be cutting so close to the bone, reducing all she
held dear, all she'd been working for, to rubble.

And not when she was on the brink of falling for
him—a tumble she was going to have to find a way to halt.

She had room in her life for a fling, not for a romance. Especially not for a romance that would leave her brokenhearted. How could it not when after next week he wouldn't even be around?

She saw how miserable April and Evan were when they went a day without seeing each other. If she and Quentin were to become involved, their schedules would keep them apart for weeks, months even.

That was not her idea of a relationship.

As much as she'd hated working in the Thirsty Rattler, she'd loved the end of the day shift, when her brother's wife Shelly would come to pick him up and take him home.

The gleam in Matt's eyes at seeing his woman had never failed to prick Shandi's heart with envy. She'd so wanted what they had, found herself insanely covetous of what they shared.

Thing was, she wanted it all.

The relationship, the career. A man loving her as wholly as she loved him. Clients clamoring for her services. Until she was fighting off her own groupies. Oh, but for the exposure.

Wouldn't that show her family that she wasn't wasting her time reaching for the stars? That she had talent for more than drawing a beer, pouring shots and spinning whiskey bottles as if she'd walked off the set of *Coyote Ugly?*

Pushing aside thoughts of her family, she returned to the present and admitted that taking off tonight and inviting Quentin into her home was more risky than embarking on their affair.

Sexually they were equals. Professionally she was a novice to his seasoned performer. At least April and Evan would be here to cushion the fall should Quentin drop her. And really, wasn't that what she was expecting?

She was doing what the Mrs. Cypruses of the world did. Using him for what he could do for her. Why wouldn't he tell her to take a hike as he had with all the others?

Uh, maybe because you've got something more going on with him than that, girlfriend?

No, she didn't. She couldn't. It was a fun fling, an affair. He'd said so himself. That was all.

He'd tie up his business early next week, finish the last of the meetings that were the only reason he was in the city and then he'd leave Hush and leave her.

And because she wasn't ready to deal with that, she got back to the reason she was here.

Standing in the kitchen that opened right off the living room, chicken breasts pounded flat on the cutting board next to the sink, a mixture of spinach, ricotta, eggs and mozzarella in one bowl, seasoned bread crumbs in another, she set to work assembling ingredients.

She knew how to cook, she just rarely did—and was nervous the lack of practice was going to show. At least, until thirty minutes later, when she found her stomach growling from the aroma of chicken, oregano, basil and fresh garlic bread filling the air.

Now if everyone would get here so she could eat, she thought as she tossed the mixed greens for the salad.

The doorbell rang, as if on cue.

She hooked the utensils on the rim of the salad bowl, smoothed down the gauzy white toga-style shift she wore with Roman sandals and prayed it was April and Evan—though she knew it wouldn't be.

Evan lived here. He had a key and no need to ring for entrance. Quentin, on the other hand...

They hadn't talked since the middle of the night, that conversation filled with uncertainty and lust and frustration. The desperate need to understand what was happening gnawing at both of them. The desire that was more than physical need binding them. She took a deep breath and opened the door.

His suit was a deep chocolate, almost black, the brown noticeable only because of the way she saw strands of the same color woven through his hair.

He wore it down, and it skimmed his shoulders, that soft lion's mane of chestnut and coffee hiding beneath the blond.

She curled her fingers into her palms and invited him to come in. "I like your hair down."

He handed her a bottle of Chablis and a bouquet of six daisies that made her smile. "I like what you've done with your face."

Tonight she'd used silver paint, gold flecks and black kohl to create a Greek-goddess look. It had taken her hours. Having him notice made every minute, every used sponge, brush and tissue worth it. "Thanks. I like showing off."

He laughed at that. "You do a damn good job. And the honesty doesn't hurt."

"I hope not," she said, returning to the kitchen and searching in a lower cabinet for the cobalt-blue bud vase that was the only one she had. "What you see is what you get. Well, except for the lie of the makeup."

"Ah, so you're hiding behind a veneer of what?" he asked with a suspicious lift of one brow. "Exaggeration? Half-truths?"

She straightened to find him standing directly in front of her, the corners of his eyes crinkling with the laughter he held in. "Actually this would be MAC Studio Tech NC 15, along with Sea Me and Electric Eel."

"Touché," he said, offering her a smile that had her melting like the cheese in her spinach and chicken. "Food smells great."

"I hope it tastes great." She carried the flowers to the table set with cantaloupe-, avocado- and plum-colored flea market Fiestaware knockoffs. The vase fit right in. "We also have salad and bread, and the corkscrew's hanging on the side of the fridge if you want—"

His hands at her waist, he spun her around and into his body. She gasped as her breath was crushed from her lungs, her hands curling into the fabric of the tan dress shirt he wore sans tie.

She slid her hands up to cup his nape and slowly lifted her gaze, caught by his tongue wetting his lower lip, by his eyes that sizzled.

"I want to kiss you, but I don't want to ruin your face," he said, stroking a hand over her hair that hung straight down her back past her shoulders.

"You won't." She raised up to her tiptoes, dropped a

kiss on his lips. "As long as you keep it sweet and simple and save the tongue for later."

He leaned down, smiling, nibbling at her mouth. "Does that mean there's going to be a later?"

"We probably should wait and see." She kissed him, rubbed her nose against his, threaded her fingers through the strands of his hair. "You may hit the door at a run once I tell you about my class project."

"Not a chance." He slid his hands to the small of her back and pressed her close, kneaded the muscles there. "You've got my curiosity up."

"Be careful there," she whispered against his mouth, "or it's going to be more than your curiosity we have to worry about."

"There's a reason I haven't let you take my coat."

She felt the heat of the blush she knew was staining her face with a rosy pink glow. "You mean, besides the fact that I'm hopeless as a hostess?"

Quentin leaned forward, nuzzled the skin beneath her ear. "You're good in bed. That's all that matters."

"Is it?" She pulled away, staring intently into his eyes as she did. "Because Mrs. Cyprus can always help you out if that's the case."

"You know it's not," he said gruffly, reaching down to slap her on the ass. "And if you say anything about that woman again, I'm afraid I'll have to turn you over my knee."

"Promises, promises," she replied and had just slipped her own hand to his backside to return the spanking favor when the door opened and Evan and April walked in.

"Uh, is this a bad time?" Evan asked. "Because I'm pretty sure we were invited for dinner. No one said anything about seeing a show."

Laughing, Shandi pushed away from Quentin, though she didn't argue when he kept hold of her hand. She gestured with her free one. "Quentin Marks, this is my roommate, Evan Harcourt, and our shared girlfriend, April Carter."

"April, Evan." Quentin let her go and extended his hand to shake the others'. "It's nice to meet you both."

"As it is you," April said. "I can see why Shandi's been keeping you a secret."

Shandi sputtered and headed for the kitchen and the corkscrew about which she'd so quickly forgotten. "I haven't been keeping anything or anyone a secret. Good grief, Quentin and I only met this week."

He followed her, took the corkscrew from her hand and nodded toward the wineglasses hanging from the stemware rack beneath one of the cabinets, glancing at April as he said, "It just *seems* like we've known each other forever."

And it did, Shandi mused, sliding four of the eight glasses free. Especially when they were already communicating silently and working together without a hitch, teasing their way through a task as simple as opening and pouring wine.

"Yeah," she said, setting the first two glasses on the countertop. "The newness is already wearing off. Boredom setting in and all that stuff."

Evan pulled out one of the kitchen chairs and sat. "So

that groping we saw when we came in was about putting the spark back into the relationship, huh?"

April gasped. "Evan!"

Quentin winked at Shandi, sending a thrill to her toes.

"Something like that. We were trying out one of those *Cosmo* tip things."

"Right," Quentin said. "'Ten Ways to Spice Up Your Kitchen.'"

Shandi held out the second set of glasses, her hands trembling a bit as Quentin wrapped his over hers and poured. Passing those off to the other couple, she picked up the glass Quentin had filled for her, met his eyes over the rim as she sipped. He did the same, the sharp intensity of his gaze making it hard for her to swallow.

She had no idea how she was going to manage to make it through this entire meal—much less the evening—if he didn't stop with the sexy, smoky I-know-what-you-look-like-naked looks.

Except those weren't the looks that were giving her the most grief.

What she was having trouble dealing with was how he saw beyond her mask to her soul that tonight felt inordinately fragile.

Setting her glass on the table because she suddenly needed space, she motioned for April's help. "If you'll grab the bread out of the oven, I'll finish the salad and we can get started here."

"It smells fabulous," April said.

"Agreed," Quentin added.

"And since neither April or I cook," Evan said, turning in his seat to set his glass next to his plate and catching April's eye, "we'll have to pick up extra slack at the new place and let you feed us."

Shandi looked from her roommate to her girlfriend who was suddenly busy slicing bread. "What new place?"

"The one the three of us are going to move into."

QUENTIN WASN'T SURE WHEN he'd shared a better home-cooked meal or sat down to one more interesting. Evan's moving announcement had caught Shandi totally off guard.

Rather strange that her roommate would announce such a decision in front of a disinterested audience, but then what did Quentin know about the relationship Shandi shared with the other couple?

Meeting the two, he would have thought April to be the roommate and Evan to be the visiting boyfriend. That wasn't the case at all.

From what Quentin had managed to gather before the subject had been dropped, Evan's grandmother owned the apartment he and Shandi shared and allowed them to live rent free since their relationship was platonic.

Though the details were fuzzy, never having been completely spelled out, it appeared Shandi was going to have to come up with cash she didn't have for rent and living expenses for a move she clearly didn't want to make.

He couldn't blame her, standing as he was in her kitchen that reminded him of the set from *Friends* and pouring her another glass of wine.

They were alone again at last, the other couple having left after the four of them had worked together to clean the kitchen. Shandi hadn't said much while scraping dishes and loading the dishwasher.

He could tell her mind was elsewhere, no doubt calculating her schedule and her finances, time taken away from school in order to move, extra time put in at work to afford the change.

Picking up both of their glasses and crossing the room to where she stood in front of the wall of windows looking out into the night, he realized they never had talked about her class project.

The evening's conversation had instead been casual banter sprinkled with queries about his career and several stilted references to Evan's announcement.

It was time for a distraction, he decided, handing her the wine. "Not a bad view except for the buildings in the way."

"Funny guy," she said, taking the glass and holding it close but not drinking. "I'm looking at the sky. Or what I can see of it anyway."

From here there wasn't much. A few stars was all. A sliver of moon. "What's on the roof of the building?"

She thought for a moment, then shrugged. "I don't know. I've never been up there."

"So? Let's go."

She glanced over. "To the roof?"

"Why not? More sky to see from up there." He held out a hand. She hesitated briefly but then took it.

They made their way to the apartment's front door, where she grabbed her keys off a hook beside it, locked up and showed him the way to the building's stairwell.

Four flights later and they walked out onto the rooftop, where Shandi was surprised to find a vegetable garden flourishing in one corner between rows of potted palms that eerily complemented her costume.

"Wow. I had no idea," she said and laughed softly in that way she had that reminded him of crystal clear bells. "I've been spending all that time at the apartment window after work when I could've been unwinding up here."

"Except I doubt being up here alone in the middle of the night would be particularly smart."

"Well, yeah. I know that. I wasn't being literal." She shrugged. "Just dreaming."

She struck him as too practical and focused to dream. She was diligently working at her job and toward her degree; both played a part in the pursuit of her career. Dreaming didn't fit the profile. "Do you dream a lot?"

She sputtered. "Who has time?" That matched his assessment, but then she added, "Or enough time, I guess I should ask, because I'll admit to doing my fair share."

And just when he thought he knew her. "What do you dream about?"

She rolled her shoulders, sipped her wine, crossed in front of him to step underneath the palms, looking as if she belonged on the set of a movie, *Troy* or *Alexander* or even *Cleopatra*. "A Tony, an Oscar for Best Makeup. Just your average makeup artist's dream."

He chuckled when he really felt like groaning at the tension drawing his body tight. She was so stunning, so beautiful. And he loved that she made him laugh. "Okay, I'll give you that."

"As if you have any say in my dreams?" She gave him a look over the rim of her glass as she sipped, then shook back her hair and sighed. "What am I saying? *I* obviously have no input in where I *live,* forget controlling my fantasy life."

He'd wondered about that, how close to the surface her vulnerability ran. "Is that going to be tough on you? Moving and paying rent?"

"Name me one struggling-artist-student type in this city who doesn't have it tough."

She glanced over at him, the moon turning everything about her—her hair, her clothes, the makeup on her face—to a silvery-white. A delicate, ethereal, near gossamer mix of stars and moon.

"Never mind," she said moments later. "I doubt there are many of us who run in your circles."

He glanced down and considered the glint of light off his own glass of wine. "Are you calling me a snob?"

"No, I'm being a realist," she said as a breeze rustled the palms and lifted the hem of her dress and a few strands of her hair. "And I'm pissed that my two best friends have put me in this situation. If they've decided to bite the bullet and move in together, why didn't they include me on the plans? It's not like I'm a totally un-involved bystander here."

"Doesn't seem very bestfriend-like," he mused, drinking again because he was having hell with all the things she was making him feel. "But that's just me looking down from the loft of my ivory tower."

"Figures you wouldn't be content with an average tower. Nope, gotta have a loft." A dry smile spread over her mouth before she seemed to deflate. "I'm sorry. None of that came out the way I wanted it to."

"Then why don't you explain it to me," he said, because he wanted to know her, what made her tick, what she was going to do now that she'd been dealt this blow.

"Okay," she agreed, raising one finger of the hand holding her wineglass. "But only if you agree that I get to call in the marker anytime I want."

"What marker?"

"I give you a piece of who I am, you have to do the same. And," she rushed to amend, "by *piece* I don't mean sex."

He'd always kept his past to himself, his private life private. So it made no sense that the idea of revealing to Shandi what she wanted to know wasn't all wrapped up in that same shield of self-preservation.

But what he told her or didn't was moot anyway. He was leaving next week, a thought that caused a strange pang to the center of his chest. "Sure. Why not?"

She twisted back and forth, as if shaking her whole body and not only her head, while she considered him. "Hmm. That was too easy."

The woman wouldn't give an inch. He walked closer. "You'd rather I said no?"

She stopped twisting, stared into her glass as she ran a finger around the rim. "It would be easier to believe you if you did."

Touché, he mused and shrugged. "It's a wall I've lived behind a long time."

"Would letting someone in be such a bad thing?" she asked softly, lifting her gaze.

It took the strength of a thousand men to make the admission she was forcing from him. "I'm pretty sure that's what I'm doing here."

"And?" she asked moments later, moments during which he wondered what was wrong with his heart. God, but it burned as if it had been pierced, and pierced hard. "Is it so terribly frightening?"

To let down his guard? To trust that her attentions were real? To know he wasn't stepping off into a situation that would do more damage than the paternity suit?

No. It wasn't. Not frightening in the least.

And it felt damn good to realize that he believed in her and in the things she made him feel.

He raised a hand and cupped her cheek that was cooled by the night air. The light of the moon kissed her bare arms, and he watched her gooseflesh rise. "Are you cold?"

She shivered. "No. Nervous but not cold."

"What do you have to be nervous about?" he asked as he slid his fingers to her nape.

She shuddered again. "The responsibility."

His frown deepened. "Of what?"

"You."

At that he tossed back his head and laughed. "You make me sound like a new puppy."

"It's a workable analogy," she said, leaning into him once he wrapped an arm around her shoulders. "You've got those eyes that beg for attention."

"More like you've been seeing your own eyes reflected back."

"Hmph. My eyes do not beg."

"Maybe not." Her annoyance amused him—especially since she'd mumbled the words into his chest. He found himself lighthearted and enjoying the rare-to-him feeling. "But your mouth certainly does."

"What did I tell you?" she moved away, putting enough distance between them that he felt the loss. "We're not up here to talk about sex."

"Hmm. All this talk of puppies and eyes, I'm not sure I remember what we *are* up here to talk about." He shoved his hands into his pockets, knowing exactly why they'd left the apartment and come.

For the change of scenery Shandi needed, the fresh air and the break from the place it looked as if she wouldn't be calling home for much longer.

But suddenly he didn't want to talk about any of that.

He wanted to change the subject, to see the light return to her eyes, to feel the heat from her fire that burned when her passions ran high.

He watched her walk along the low brick wall edging the garden. "Though, now that I think about it, wasn't it something to do with a class project?"

She hung her head, shook it. "I'm about ready to blow off the whole thing. I can't even think about it now."

He joined her where she'd dropped to sit on the bricks, breathing in the smells of rich peat and fertile ground and cooling tar. "That doesn't sound like the Shandi I know. Giving up after being so excited?"

She glanced over, her eyes limned in smudged kohl, her lashes heavy and dark over the shimmering silver of her mask. "You think you know me that well? After less than a week of interrupted conversations and equally abbreviated, uh, intimate encounters?"

He didn't even stop to think. He simply nodded. "Yeah. I do. That phone call this morning said a lot."

"Dear Lord, Quentin," she said, leaning against him. "How can everything be going right one minute and the next minute it all be ripped away?"

Because that's life, the cynical bastard in him wanted to say. Instead he wrapped one arm around her, held her close and whispered, "Because, Shandi Fossey, that's how you find out what you're made of."

"Easy for you made-of-money types to say. Us not-made-of-money types have to cut back on classes, work extra shifts, possibly get second jobs, just to pay rent. Forget utilities or entertainment or clothes."

"You'll do fine," he said, unable to imagine her doing anything but landing on her feet.

She rocked against him. "It's a damn good thing

Chef's generous with his handouts. At least I won't starve."

"I won't let you starve."

"Oh, what?" She pulled back enough to look into his face as she interrogated him. "Now you're a patron of starving student-artists?"

He hadn't considered it before, but... "I could be, sure. Have my accountant set up a scholarship fund. Or a grant. To take care of your expenses so you could concentrate on school full-time."

She continued to stare up at him, her gaze hard to define in the eerie glow of the moon. But then she blinked slowly, her mouth drawn in a thin line that even a blind man couldn't mistake for a smile. "You would do that? For me?"

"I've thought about doing something like it for a while now," he lied, having carefully weighed the answer and finding he didn't like the truth.

He'd been so wrapped up in his own career, he'd never thought of giving back until now. Until meeting this amazing woman whom he wanted to see succeed.

This woman who hadn't asked him for a thing except to help her with a project she still hadn't told him about.

Leaving her wineglass on the brick wall, Shandi got to her feet slowly, turned and stared down.

He could almost see the wisps of steam coming from her ears as she towered above.

"So you'd support me while I went to school, and the only thing I'd have to do in return is sleep with you?"

9

IS THAT WHAT HE MEANT? That he wanted to set her up as his mistress? A kept woman?

Did he think calling himself a patron of the arts instead of a sugar daddy would make it palatable for the both of them?

She couldn't believe it. She could *not* believe it and she began to pace. Sure, they'd known each other less than a week, but she had never picked up a single clue that this was how he operated.

Especially since his suggestion was nothing but the converse of his objection to being pursued because of his reputation. Instead he was *using* his reputation, his success, to get what *he* wanted.

But then he surged to his feet and spat out his next words. "Hell, no, that's not what I meant. Why would you think so?"

"Honestly?" She crossed her arms tightly over her chest, holding in the crushing sense of suffocation. "Because the idea seemed to come out of nowhere. As if it suddenly occurred to you that you could have me whenever you wanted as long as you were paying my way."

"The idea did come out of nowhere, Shandi, but that sure as hell was not the intent behind it," he said, moving forward and kicking the wineglass he'd left on the ground. It shattered, and he bit off a long string of foul words.

"I'm sorry. I'll replace it. And, no. That is not an attempt to buy my way into your bed." He headed for the door to the staircase, opened it and stood back waiting for her to join him before he walked down.

Staring at him as he did, watching the play of light over his face, she had no idea why that one act of thoughtfulness—his waiting for her, not wanting to leave her alone on the rooftop no matter how deeply he felt her insult—did her in.

But it did. She sank back to where she'd been sitting and buried her face in her hands. She didn't cry; she hadn't yet reached the point of total meltdown, though she was certain it was next on the agenda.

Across the roof the staircase door clicked shut with a resounding echo. Quentin's footsteps scuffed over the loose-gravel-and-tar surface as he made his way back to the garden wall where she sat.

He didn't join her, but she sensed him standing there, still waiting, probably wondering what the hell craziness he'd gotten himself into and how he could extricate himself without having to make excuses beyond saying goodbye.

She raised her head, shook it, sighed. "If I read something into your offer that wasn't there, I apologize. I can only blame it on the moon."

He shifted from one foot to the other before serving back her words for more explanation. "The moon?"

She nodded, feeling stupid and silly, both of which were better than feeling as if she'd ruined everything. "I'm used to the tiny bit of the sky I can see from my window. All these moonbeams are getting to me."

Since she was staring at his shoes, she saw the minute he turned, tugged up on the knees of his pants as he sat beside her. He left enough distance between them that one of them had to make the first move.

So she did, gathering up the material of her dress so as not to snag it and scooting near. "I'm sorry. Truly. I think I snapped because your offer presents the perfect answer to all my problems but I just can't take it."

"I know that." He laced his hands between his spread knees, hung his head. "You wouldn't be who you are if you took the easy way out."

"Then why did you do it?" *Why did you give me a glimpse of hope?* she wanted to add, but didn't.

"I'm not sure," he admitted. "Maybe trying to buy my way out of my cynical bastardy."

She smiled to herself. "Hmm. I'm not sure that's the correct use of that word."

"What can I say?" he asked with a snort of self-deprecation. "When you're around, I'm a tongue-tied idiot."

Her smile deepened, reaching down to squeeze her heart. "Really? I do that to you?"

He reached over and took one of her hands in his, as

if the simple contact of palms pressed close said everything. "You do more than you'll ever realize."

"Tell me," she said, squeezing his fingers and waiting breathlessly to hear what he said. Because she hadn't told him the whole truth earlier. This week her dreams had been all about him.

But it wasn't going to be that easy, she realized as he shook his head. "Nope. Not until you tell me about this class project that you're not going to dump."

"Okay." If she blurted it out rather than dragging it the way she'd been doing, at least the wait for his reaction would be over.

She breathed deeply and said, "I have to do a print ad for a hair-color product. I'm using April and Kit Prescott as my models."

"Kit from Hush?" he asked after several seconds passed.

"Right. The brunette and the blonde. Perfect bookends."

"No black?"

She shook her head. "Too harsh. April has a gentle warmth, like buttered toast. And Kit is bright, like eggs sunny-side up. Weird, I know," she went on, gesturing with one hand, "but it works for what I'm wanting to do. Except I've always known I need more. That the contrast isn't quite right."

"And this is where you want to use me."

"Yes. Your coloring is the perfect amalgamation of Kit's and April's," she explained, wondering if he thought she was totally nuts or if she should mention how wild and sexy he would look standing between the two serenely poised women. "The bookends and all the pages in between."

"You're back to books, and I'm stuck on breakfast," he said, shaking his head.

"Hey, I make my art with cosmetics, not with words." And then she groaned. "Which sucks because I'm going to have to come up with a slogan that works and I'm pretty sure eggs and toast won't."

"They work for breakfast," he said, getting to his feet and pulling her with him. She straightened her dress.

"Breakfast?" Was he putting her off or was he simply wanting an invitation to spend the night? She took a stab in the dark. "I have to be at school at eight. I don't do breakfast."

"You will tomorrow," he said and tugged her across the rooftop to the stairs. "My treat."

"Are you taking me out or cooking?" she asked as he opened the stairwell door.

"Depends. Do you want to get up early or sleep in and have breakfast in bed?" The door closed with a snap, leaving them with only the light from the sputtering bulb on the floor below by which to see.

He moved to stand on the step beneath the main landing—a move that put him at her eye level. She stayed where she was and looked into his face, lifting a hand and caressing him, the smooth skin over his perfect cheekbones.

Why couldn't he have been a doctor, a lawyer, any profession with roots in this city she was making her home? "Thank you. For forgiving me. For understanding."

He turned his face to kiss the center of her palm, nuzzling the bristle of his goatee against her. "You've got a lot at stake. A lot on your mind. I should've been more clear with my intentions."

"I shouldn't have jumped to conclusions," she said, threading her fingers back over his ear and into the thick silk of his hair. It slid like water over her wrists, and she felt her nipples tighten.

With her white dress picking up all the stairwell's light, Quentin noticed. He buried his face between her breasts and breathed in, settling his hands over her ribs, pressing his thumbs upward.

Her hands found his shoulders. Holding on, she closed her eyes and drank up the sensations sweetening her body, thinking how much better this would be in bed. *Or not,* she mused, as he found the garment's overly large and loose armholes and touched her skin.

She shuddered as the hair at her nape tingled. "You never did tell me if you intended to serve me breakfast in your bed or mine?"

"Do you have a preference?" He breathed his question into the hollow of her throat, his thumbs rubbing circles over her bare nipples.

Clenching her thighs and the muscles of her sex, she tried to answer but couldn't speak until she'd cleared her throat. "Mine's closer."

"That settles it then. We'll stay here." He kissed his way from her neck to her shoulders before moving down a step and taking his attentions lower, breathing hotly over the gauze of her dress where it covered her breasts, her waist, until he was on his knees and his breath puffed over her thighs. "As long as you have eggs."

She didn't, she realized as she widened her stance, the pit of her belly burning. She'd used them all for dinner. "I have pancake mix. Add water and pour."

"That'll work." He lifted her skirt. She reached for the hand railing and held on as he pushed aside the minimal barrier of her thong, opened his mouth and kissed her as intimately as a woman could be kissed.

She trembled, gasped, couldn't believe this was happening, that the fire between them burned this hotly, this fiercely and with such a desperate need to be fed that what they were doing seemed the only logical course.

He parted the lips of her sex with his thumbs, licked his way through her folds, found her entrance and pushed his tongue inside and did it while capturing her clit between his thumbs and massaging it.

She cried out, bit back the rest of the sound, feared she wasn't going to be able to stand because he'd replaced his tongue with two of his fingers and was now sucking her as he stroked.

"Quentin, wait. We need to go downstairs. I don't... think...I have any syrup."

He chuckled there where his lips and tongue and fingers were busy making a wet, juicy mess between her legs. And she really hated putting a stop to what he was doing, but she wanted more. To feel the weight of his body, his mouth on hers, his thick sex inside.

As if he'd been reading her mind, he left her with one last lingering kiss, and as she shivered and groaned with the pleasure, he got to his feet, stepped up to where she was waiting and turned her to face the door.

She pressed her body to the cool metal, listened as Quentin's zipper came down, spread her legs and waited. She didn't give a damn about syrup. Not when he made her feel as if her only two choices were to come or to die.

Her skirt up to her waist, her thong a scrap of nothing he ripped away, he moved in behind her, bent at the knees, found his position and thrust upward. He nearly took her off her feet when he did.

She bit her lip until she tasted blood, trying to keep quiet, to hold in the cries that ripped through her—a useless endeavor. How could she be silent when every time he drove into her he shook with the pleasure he felt?

He moved one hand to her hip, slid the other around to her stomach, his cheek rubbing against her hair as he whispered into her ear words she'd never heard him speak, words describing what he loved about her body, what he wanted to do to her, what he wanted her to do to him.

She wanted all of it. She wanted everything.

She wanted him—in her bed, in her body. But most of all she wanted him in her life. She wanted to laugh with him and cry with him and share her troubles as she worked them through. She wanted to open her eyes to him in the morning, kiss him before she went to sleep at night.

The realization tore through her, overwhelming her, and she cried out as she came. Quentin followed, spilling himself inside her, his low throaty growl tickling her ear, his body warm where he'd pressed himself against her back.

Caught between his warmth and the cool metal door, she collapsed, exhausted, thankful he was there to keep her from sliding all the way to the ground. Long moments later, he pulled free from her body, adjusting her dress over her hips before stepping back and putting himself together.

She turned, leaned against the door, her hands stacked behind her. "I think we have a problem."

"It's good to hear you say that because I was thinking it was just me." He didn't look up until he'd finished slipping the extra length of his belt through its loop. When he did, she swore she saw sadness in his eyes. "But I'm clueless what to do about it."

She wanted to know what he was thinking, what that sadness meant.

She didn't want to be the only one suffering here, dealing with an upheaval to her life that reduced the struggles of work and school and finances to dust beneath her feet.

Because that's what this felt like, this attraction that was consuming them both.

"I suppose we can let it burn itself out," she said,

brushing by him and starting down the stairs, not realizing until she reached the landing below that he hadn't yet followed.

Swallowing what felt like a ball of fluttering wings, she looked up. "Quentin?"

He descended slowly, his gaze holding hers as he made his way to where she stood. And he didn't stop once he'd reached her but advanced. She retreated into the corner until she had nowhere to go or to run or to hide.

He stared into her eyes, a predator considering his prey. "Do you think that's all this is, Shandi? A flash fire that will burn itself out?"

What was she supposed to tell him? That she didn't want it to, hoped it never would? That the idea of being kept by him appealed on countless levels when she should find it too offensive to appeal on any?

But she didn't know how much of that, if any, she wanted to say, and so she told him the rest of the truth. "I don't think it is, no. But I hope it does. I can't spend my life waiting for you to come to town, feeling complete only when you're here, feeling alive only when we're together.

"I don't want to live that way. I wouldn't be able to respect myself. And if that's what you wanted from me, I wouldn't respect you either."

"So? DID QUENTIN SPEND THE night?" April asked, hurrying after Shandi as she headed toward the subway station, hiking her backpack up farther on her shoulder.

"And just what business is that of yours?" she answered, glancing to the side where her best friend carried a Prada bag and nothing more. "By the way, Evan wasn't home when I left for class this morning."

"That's because I talked him into staying over last night." April sidestepped a bike messenger whizzing by, then hurried to catch up, her Jimmy Choo slides clicking on the sidewalk. "I knew you wouldn't want him to be a third wheel on your cozy bicycle built for two."

"That's a horrible analogy." Though she and Quentin *had* gone for quite a ride once they'd returned to the apartment from the roof.

And, eww. Seemed she wasn't doing so good today in the analogy department herself. Or the walking department. Or in the emotions department.

She hated admitting it, but since Quentin had left this morning, she'd become a real crab. He'd kept her so warm during the night; she couldn't remember ever sleeping so soundly, so comfortably.

Her bed had felt way too empty when she'd finally gotten up and she'd felt way too alone.

She hated that now she was taking it all out on her best friend. "You might consider taking a creative writing class. Or at least work on your originality, especially since that gallery you're planning is supposed to showcase April Carter originals."

"Stop changing the subject," April said, grabbing hold of Shandi's backpack strap and jerking her to a stop. "And stop being a bitch. I was talking about you

and Quentin. Not my analogical skills or my originality."

"Well, I was talking about you and Evan. Quentin
and I are only having a fling," Shandi said, wondering
why today it pained her to say that when yesterday it
hadn't been so hard. "What you have with Evan is supposed to be more. It gets top conversational billing."

"What do you mean my relationship with Evan is
supposed to be more? It *is* more." April crossed her
arms, lifted her chin and tried to look down her nose—
not an easy task when she was four inches shorter.

Shandi sighed. She wanted to get home. To soak in
a tub until her skin couldn't be any softer. To do her toenails, her hair, to shave and wax any sign of stubble. To
get over this cranky mood.

To decide what to wear beneath her uniform tonight
in case Quentin was struck with the urge to undress her.
They had only a handful of days left to spend together.
She wanted them to be all they could be.

What she didn't want was to get into this argument
now when she was so grouchy. But it wasn't fair to bail
on April. She'd still be a big part of Shandi's life after
Quentin was gone.

She hadn't had a chance to talk to either her current
or future roommate since Evan had dropped his bomb,
and they needed to have this discussion. Especially considering it looked as though they were going to be sharing an apartment soon.

She glanced at the clogged intersection she'd have
to fight her way through to get to the downtown side of

the subway station, then glanced back to where April was waiting. The decision was a no-brainer. "Let's go get coffee, okay?"

April nodded without saying a word, then hooked her arm through Shandi's. Instead of crossing the street at the corner, they turned and headed for the Starbucks where Evan worked.

Today being Friday, he wasn't scheduled until after his last class let out at four. She and April had plenty of private time to talk.

Once April had ordered a nonfat, extra hot vanilla latte and Shandi an espresso straight up, the two managed to grab a just-vacated table near the front window. Once they were settled, Shandi jumped right in.

"What I want to know is how you and Evan think the three of us are going to be able to afford an apartment with more than one room or four hundred square feet when only two of us have part-time jobs."

April wrapped both hands around the green logo on her cup and stared down. "Well, obviously I'm going to have to get one, too—"

"You mean you're going to have to get *two,* too." Shandi couldn't help it. Her exasperation and frustration were both showing their ugly heads. "I'm going to have to cut back on classes and take on extra shifts.

"If I can't get the hours I need at Erotique, I'll have to find a second job. So will Evan. It's going to push all of our degrees back another semester at least. Did y'all not talk about any of this?"

"Of course we did," April said, sipping her latte and

avoiding Shandi's gaze while a jazzy-sounding reggae poured from the coffee shop's speakers.

Well, they were just going to have to talk about it again, Shandi resolved. And talk about it with her. "Why wasn't I included? It's hardly fair that you've made this decision without even talking to me about it. It's not like you're the only two involved here."

"Actually we are." April looked up, her gaze tighter, determined. "Evan and I want to be together. We want to make it as a couple on our own."

"On your own as long as I'm there to help, you mean," Shandi said, glaring as another customer walked through and jarred her elbow without an apology. When Shandi returned her gaze to April, she was shaking her head.

"If you want to be there with us to share expenses, we'd love it. But this isn't about you, Shandi. It's about us." April sat straighter in her chair, as if testing out her new backbone. "It's taken a while, but I finally get what you've been telling me all this time."

"What's that?" Shandi asked, feeling small and selfish but still worried about everything this upheaval would mean, wondering how old she would be when she finally finished school, wondering how long she could carry a heavier schedule and not collapse from the weight.

"We can't make our lives all about pleasing our families, which is exactly what we've both been doing," April admitted, toying with the lid on her cup. "At first it was a compromise, but now it's a sacrifice. We're giving up what *we* want so that his grandmother and my parents will be happy. I don't know why it took us so long to wake up to that truth."

How could Shandi argue when the words were the ones she'd repeatedly served up to her girlfriend?

She slumped back, feeling way too tired to deal with a full shift at the bar tonight. "You could've told me at least that you were thinking about this instead of springing it on me in front of Quentin."

"Trust me, Evan is still hurting from me beating him up about that," April said. "It only came up the night before. Or I guess it was actually that same morning. I couldn't sleep and went out to the living room. We talked about a lot of the stuff you've been telling me we needed to deal with. I doubt Evan thought about Quentin being there. He just wanted to share the good news."

"It is good news, really." Shandi was happy for the couple. Admittedly not so happy for herself, but her friend was right.

This wasn't about her, and making it so was dumping on April's happiness. "I'm glad for you, truly. I just wish it didn't mean we all have to move. I love that apartment almost as much as I love not paying for it."

April laughed. "I know. And actually we're hoping I'm the only one who has to move."

April's words floated by like a life buoy and Shandi grabbed on. "He's going to talk to his grandmother?"

"Soon, yes. First I'm going to get a job. If we end up having to move, I'll need one anyway." April swirled the remains of her coffee in her cup, glanced briefly at a trio of giggling teen girls flirting with the barista. "Mrs. Harcourt's biggest objection to us being together is that coming from money has meant I haven't had to work."

Shandi sipped her coffee, arched a brow. "I thought her biggest objection was that living with Evan meant you would be living in sin."

April's mouth twisted into a grin. "That's why we thought we'd offer her a token rent payment and tell her I'm bunking with you as I work my way to full independence."

Shandi let go a chuckle. "You think she'll buy that?"

"I doubt it." April laughed. Laughed harder when Shandi joined her. "So our next option is to get married."

At that Shandi stopped laughing. "What? You'd get married just so you could move in?"

"No, silly." A warm blush softened April's face. "We'd get married because we're in love and want to spend the rest of our lives together."

Shandi was aghast. She couldn't even fathom. "What about all the plans you've made? Hell, the plans Evan has made? Your gallery, his drawing his way around the world? The monstrously expensive wedding you're going to force your parents to pay for and will take months to organize?"

"A big wedding would be fun, but I don't have to have one. And being married doesn't mean giving up any of our plans." April cocked her head to the side. "Why would you think it did?"

Because that's what had happened to every girlfriend

she'd had back in Round-Up? Because every female member of the Fossey family had abandoned her own dreams for what her husband determined to be the family's good?

Shandi drained the rest of her coffee, reached for her backpack she'd set on the floor at her feet. "I've seen it too much, I guess. Watched too many friends from school give up their dreams to family demands."

"That's why you came here, isn't it?" April asked, slipping the strap of her bag from her chair. "You've never told me that before."

Shandi shrugged. She needed to get home. She had work to get ready for, and it had been too long since she'd seen Quentin. "The why doesn't matter. Just that I'm doing what I have to do to get where I want to be. Same as you are. And Evan. The same as Quentin did."

April turned, started to get up from her chair, then stopped and looked over with an expression of curious regard. "Is that why you like him? Because he went after what he wanted and got there in such a big way?"

"I don't know if it's that, or just that he is who he is." Ugh, but that sounded so lame. "I'm not even sure that makes any sense. I mean, I'd hope I wouldn't be so shallow as to be attracted to his power. And that's not even it. It's more about his success."

"Isn't that the same thing?"

Exasperated, Shandi sighed. "I wish I could put it into words. He went after his dream. He never gave up. He made himself into who he is with hard work. His own two hands. I can't help but admire that."

"I'd say it's more like you identify with that. Two of a kind and all."

"I suppose, yeah. Plus, he doesn't use his reputation or his success to get what he wants. He still works for it. And that turns me on."

April seemed to take in all of that, then said, "I'd figure just looking at him would turn you on."

And Shandi couldn't help but grin. "Yeah. There's that, too."

10

PEOPLE, PEOPLE, PEOPLE!
Stop it already with the cocktail napkins!
Don't use them to level tables!
Don't use them for blowing your nose!
Don't use them as toys for Eartha Kitty to shred!
Or, if you do, at least CLEAN UP!
Eartha Kitty can hardly be held responsible!
Shandi

FRIDAY NIGHT FOUND QUENTIN buying drinks for an old friend, both of them lounging in leather chairs of sea-foam green at one of Erotique's low black-lacquer tables. The dropped ceiling helped to intensify the room's intimacy.

Like all of Hush, Erotique was designed to protect—perhaps even promote—anonymity. Its ambience encouraged private assignations, and that was why Quentin had chosen to meet at the bar. Or at least one of the reasons. The other being the proximity to Shandi.

Quentin faced the room while his friend sat with his back to the crowd. The arrangement worked for them both. He could look up and watch Shandi as the urge struck, and his friend could avoid a scene, since the bar's patrons as a general rule had more on their minds than stalking rock stars.

His friend was Constantine Hale of the metal band Hale's Fallen Angels. And Quentin's groupie problem was nothing compared to Constantine's.

"I wish I'd known you were in town," Connie was saying. "We could've hooked up earlier."

"Right," Quentin said with a laugh. "I'm trying to keep a low profile this trip. Hanging with you would be counterproductive."

Connie shrugged, a shock of blue-black hair falling over his forehead as he leaned forward and hooked his longneck with his index finger. "Maybe. But you can't say it wouldn't be a spitload of fun."

"I'm getting too old for your brand of fun, Hale." Smiling to himself, Quentin swirled the ice in his glass and stared down into the amber liquid, resisting the draw of the woman at the bar whose brand of fun he couldn't get enough of. "Last time you and I partied, I ended up with a paternity suit."

Connie laughed, drank again and shook his head as he swallowed. "Oh, man. If that didn't blow! I don't even remember seeing that chick that night."

"I saw her, but that was it." This time Quentin glanced at Shandi as he lifted his glass to drink. Her eyes were bright as she chatted with the couple sitting at the end of the bar where he usually sat.

His seat. His woman.

"That suit pretty much put an end to my partying days." He tucked away the possessive feelings that rose swiftly and out of nowhere and looked at Connie again. "I knew that woman was trouble when she tried to slip a demo CD into my, uh, pocket."

Connie flipped his thumb over the mouth of his bottle, playing it like an instrument. *Thwup-thwump. Thwup-thwump.* "That's the thing, man. Women. Can't live with 'em, can't wash off the stench of the sheep."

Quentin tossed back his head and laughed. "Now I *know* I'm done partying with you."

"Believe it or not, Marks, you are looking at a brand-new man," Connie said, shoving his hair back from his face so he could be seen.

"That so?" Setting his glass on the table, Quentin hoped he sounded more laid-back than he felt.

If he could sign Hale's Fallen Angels to his new label once they'd finished up with their current obligations, he'd be years ahead in his game plan. "What was your wake-up call?"

"I was losing way too many brain cells out there on the road. I'd get back home, hole up in the studio and nothing." *Thwup-thwump. Thwup-thwump. Thwup-thwump.* "I didn't much like the idea of being washed up at thirty."

Since Connie had three years to go and an unparalleled driving talent, Quentin doubted the other man would ever be washed up, but cutting back on the distractions wouldn't hurt anyone's career.

Quentin himself was the opposite end of the spectrum from any member of Hale's Fallen Angels, the one who for years wouldn't have known a distraction had it bit him on the ass.

But that didn't mean he wasn't susceptible now. And then he wondered how much of a distraction he was for Shandi, because she sure as hell was distracting him. "So what have you been working on?"

Connie's eyes lit up. "You want to hear?"

The man went nowhere without his guitar in tow, though he didn't need it to make music. He did that simply with the gift of his voice.

Quentin glanced down to where the case sat on the floor next to Connie's chair. "Sure. Be a change of pace to hear The Constantine without the Angels around."

His beer drained, Connie nodded and set the bottle on the table. He then leaned to the side and flipped the latches on the case, shifting forward in his chair and settling the guitar on his knee.

After tuning the instrument to his satisfaction, he launched into a slow, unplugged warm-up session, running through the riffs of several well-known Angels tunes.

Quentin sensed heads turning, conversation stopping, movement slowing, a hush descending.

But Connie didn't sense a thing. He was all about the music. Only the music. His eyes closed, he nodded his head in rhythm to a beat only he heard.

And then, facing Quentin, his back to the gathering audience, he sang.

"Do you know what I know
What I think
What I want
What I do when you're not around
Can I say that you know
That you sense
That you feel
That you hear me when I'm not around
Will you ever know how I know
How I fail
How I miss
How I ache when you're not around
Should I ever fear why you know
Why you hurt
Why you need
Why you cry when I'm not around"

Sitting with his elbows on his chair arms, one leg squared over the other, his hands laced and his steepled fingers tapping his chin, Quentin lifted only his eyes to search out Shandi. He wondered if she heard what he heard in Connie's song.

The pain of uncertainty and separation. The connection that even distance couldn't break. He wasn't one to grow maudlin over relationships; he'd never had a broken heart, though he'd been accused of breaking many.

He didn't wax poetic over the existence of soul mates; he had always supposed he'd enjoy the company of many women but live alone as demanded by the mistress that was his career.

As envious as he was of the wedded bliss shared by his old friends, the Tannens, in Austin, he'd never thought he'd ache to experience the same—until now.

Until Shandi.

Shandi, who stood in the corner of the bar, swaying side to side as Connie sang the ballad, a towel twisted around her fingers, which she then used to swipe at the tears in her eyes. When Quentin finally captured her gaze, the punch to his gut nearly knocked him breathless.

She was sad for him, for herself, for the two of them together. Sad because their situation meant one of them would always suffer the other not being around. Because she didn't know if they could come up with a solution that would work with their career demands.

Because she hadn't been any more prepared for him to come into her life than he'd been for her. And now here they were, this beautiful thing between them, yet neither of them knowing where to take it from here.

He found his own throat aching, his eyes burning as he turned his gaze back to Connie once Shandi stepped away to pour a drink for a customer who'd bellied up to the bar.

Connie's eyes were closed, his focus on the music, feeling it in his fingers that worked the guitar, feeling it in his soul.

"Should I ever fear why you know
Why you hurt
Why you need

Why you cry when I'm not around
Would you ever find where I know
Where I fit
Where I wait
Where I hide when you're not around
Please don't cry
Please don't ache
Please don't fear
Only imagine that I'm always around
I'll believe that you're always around"

The words ended, the music faded. Connie smiled to himself, letting what he felt settle before opening his eyes and returning from the soul of the song to the present.

Quentin gave him a solid nod of appreciation, and a second later applause rang out in the room.

Connie's expression was one of surprise, as if he'd been too deep in his head to remember he'd been singing in public, then he looked back and raised a hand to acknowledge their regard.

A moment later, his grin sheepish, he returned his guitar to its case and sat forward like a little boy seeking approval from a parent rather than a musical genius who'd turned the world of metal upside down. Clearly he had entered everyone in the bar just with the aching beauty of his singing accompanied only by a simple acoustic guitar.

Quentin reached for the glass he'd set on the table earlier. "Nice. You have more like that?"

Nodding, Connie slouched back, his hands on the

thighs he spread wide. "Three or four I'm finishing up. The band's on sabbatical for the rest of the year. The last tour nearly killed us."

Not surprising to hear considering their touring schedule. "Killed the group?"

"Nah. The group can weather anything. But we voted to a man to take the break. We're all putting things together, getting back to the basics, finding ourselves," he added with a laugh. "Crap like that."

"I hear you," Quentin said. It was like having his own thoughts looped back in stereo.

Connie pushed his hair from his eyes that didn't look old enough to know the truth of burnout. "Sergey and I hang every couple of weeks and jam on what we've written. We should be back in the studio after the first of the year."

"Are you tossing all of it into the mix?" Quentin asked, a buzz of excitement humming over his skin.

The knee Connie'd been shaking stilled. "You mean, have I thought about a solo shot?"

"Yeah. That."

"I have," he admitted hesitantly. "I'm just not sure what kind of reception The Constantine would get without the Angels backing him up."

Inclining his head, Quentin indicated the room. "I think you just saw it."

"They just enjoyed not having to pay for a show," Connie said, then winked.

The insecurity of artists never ceased to amaze. "They enjoyed you."

"Maybe." Connie shrugged. "We'll see."

"Keep me in mind."

"Truly? I'd dig working with you again."

"Then let's do it." Grinning hugely, Quentin reached out to shake the other man's hand. "I'm building a studio. In Austin. When you're ready, we'll make it happen."

They spent the rest of the night talking over old times, a life spent on the road and in the studio, how much living they'd missed out on while pursuing their passion, whether or not the end result was worth what they'd given up to get to where they were, both coming to the conclusion that they did what they did because there was nothing else they could do.

Finally Connie got up to leave. "I've got to get back before Sergey's girl locks me out. Though I think it's more about locking her big man in. I ought to stay here next time I'm in the city. I like the look."

"You want to use my room? I've got other plans for the night." Quentin glanced at his watch, looked over to see Shandi cleaning up at the bar.

Connie followed the direction of Quentin's gaze. "Hey. Nice."

Quentin didn't respond except to fish his key card from his wallet. "Leave this in the room. I'll get another from the desk tomorrow."

"Thanks, man. And seriously," Connie said, grabbing up his guitar case, "it's great to see you again. We will stay in touch."

"I'm counting on it." Quentin watched him walk off

before moving to the now-empty bar to wait for Shandi. She wasn't expecting him. They hadn't made plans to get together tonight.

In fact, they hadn't talked much at all since leaving the roof of her building. After he'd taken her like a rutting beast in the stairwell. After she'd told him she wouldn't spend her life waiting for moments they could steal.

They'd slept together last night, held each other close, but they hadn't gotten back to the part about the flash fire and how to deal with it.

Right now, however, none of that mattered because the light in the bar's back room had gone out.

He moved to the employees' door and waited. And when Shandi walked out, he wrapped an arm around her shoulders and said, "Let's go home."

QUENTIN LAY ON HIS SIDE beneath Shandi's sheets, one of her pillows punched up beneath his head.

She faced him, lying in the same position, and he watched her struggle to stay awake, to keep her eyes open and exhaustion at bay.

Once they'd finally made it to her apartment and taken care of that thing between them that couldn't wait, she'd told him she had a busy day on Saturday and if he wanted to take her out after work, he needed to let her sleep.

He had no problem with that, he'd replied seconds before she'd climbed up on top of his body for the second time.

Hard to tell the woman no when he enjoyed the way she contradicted herself as much as he enjoyed the way she took him into her body and loved him.

That had been an hour ago. She'd been drifting in and out ever since, while he'd been content to watch her.

He was feeling things that he was going to have big problems with, things that were going to make it hard to leave the city in three days when he was scheduled to fly out.

Shandi felt as vital to him as did his plans for his studio, his return to Texas, his need to extinguish the dissatisfaction that reared an ugly head of cynicism more often than he cared to admit.

And then, while he was thinking of the best way to swallow his medicine and face the fact that in a matter of days their time would be gone, her lashes fluttered up.

She pretended to glare. "I can't believe you know Constantine Hale and didn't introduce me. Or at least get me an autograph."

He lifted a brow. "You don't seem the starstruck, autograph-seeking type."

She stretched her legs, her toes seeking out and tapping against his. "I'm sleeping with you, and you don't think I'm the type to be starstruck?"

"Saucy wench, I thought you were sleeping with me because you wanted me to help you ace your class project."

She shifted on the pillow, settled deeper under the covers, smiling as she said, "I sleep with you for many reasons relating to what you can do for me."

"I see." He loved that she felt comfortable enough to tease, loved that he didn't believe anything she said.

"Hey," she said, her voice slurred with sleep. "Us starstruck groupie types are shameless about doing what we gotta do to get what we want."

"Huh. Well, it's my turn now." He slid his hand across the mattress, stroked her bare belly with his fingers. "I want something from you."

Her eyes were closed when, smiling, she lifted a brow. "Haven't I been doing something for you all night?"

She made flirting so easy, yet his time was growing short and he needed more than playful banter. He needed more than sex. Still… "I believe the doing has been mutual, cowgirl."

"Look, mister." One eye opened. "Just because I'm from outta town—"

"I was referring to the way you ride me."

"Oh. Okay." She sighed. Moved closer. Worked his hand up to her hip. "Then what do you want?"

"A simple barter. In exchange for the class project, I want something from you."

"Hmm. I'm not sure I like that. But shoot." Both eyes opened. "Oh, speaking of shoot…"

She hopped onto one elbow, the sheet sliding from her shoulders to bare her breasts. "Did I tell you we're going to use the sofa bar at the hotel? For the project shoot?"

He stayed where he was, enjoying her shift in mood, her sudden animation, the excitement that sparkled in her eyes. He had a hard time finding his voice, what with the way his chest had tightened.

And with the way he fought not to drop his gaze to her chest. "No. You didn't."

"Well, now I did," she said, smiling, her enthusiasm pouring out like warm honey onto his skin. "So what do you want?"

He levered up onto his elbow so that he faced her, so that she couldn't get away. "I want to know what you miss about Oklahoma."

That caught her off guard. He'd expected it would. She hadn't made him privy to the details, but it hadn't taken him long to learn that her family history was off-limits.

Her future was one thing; she could talk about her plans forever. But sharing where she'd come from shut her down every time.

So it didn't surprise him when she shrugged off the question with a blasé response. "Nothing, really. My family at times, I guess. Though that's more nostalgia over what could have been than what actually was."

"Then let's leave them out of it," he said. "What else do you miss? Friends? Room to breathe? Open roads?"

This time it only took her a second after she'd fallen back to the pillow and yanked the sheet to her chin to answer. "The sky."

That didn't surprise him either. "Why the sky?"

"Because the sky's the limit, of course. Whenever I'd get frustrated at work, that's what I'd tell myself. That I could do anything I wanted to do. That life wasn't all about sticking around to pour shots, because that's what's expected from the Fosseys of Round-Up."

He wondered if that was her family's way to keep members close. He asked, "All of you?"

She gave a small shrug. "Except my mother. She keeps the books, the inventory. Basically everything that doesn't require physical labor. Or throwing drunks out on their ear."

"That's your father's job?"

"And my brothers. Well, not Matt. Always the diplomat, chatting up the crowd."

She fell silent for a moment, her thoughts drawing a smile on her mouth. "Matt settled down a lot after marrying Shelly. Gave up that bad-boy Fossey image for a woman and never lived it down. Not that he cared."

"He was happy?"

"Delirious. He still is." She turned onto her side, slid her legs over to tangle with his. "He and Shelly couldn't be any cuter together. She's half his size, and he's like a big ol' puppy panting after her, stumbling over himself. They're so much in love it's intimidating."

"Intimidating?" Her skin was so smooth, so warm. He wanted so much to touch her, to love her, but she was talking and he didn't want to do anything that might shut her up. "How so?"

"Thinking if that's what love is supposed to be, that I'll never know it." Dropping her gaze, she reached over and combed her fingers through the hair on his chest. "It's so rare, what they have. And I don't want to settle."

Settle. Hmm. Things weren't looking as if they were going to go his way. "Would a long-distance relationship fall into settling?"

Her fingers stilled. "Any long-distance relationship or one in particular?"

"This one in particular," he said, wrapping his fingers around hers.

She didn't look up. "Is this a relationship?"

Here's where he had to be careful. He didn't want to scare her away or run her off or turn into the demanding, possessive caveman it would be so easy to become. "I think it could be. It's heading that way."

"Then isn't it better that we've accepted that the end is coming?" she asked, rolling away and balling up her pillow beneath her.

He hadn't accepted anything. That was the problem here. She was seeing an end when he saw only the possibilities of a beginning. "So you don't want to explore what we can do from a distance?"

"How long do you think that would last?" She closed her eyes, snorted. "We can't even make it from the roof to the sixth floor without ripping our clothes off. We'd never survive the mileage between Texas and New York."

He flopped onto his back, folded his wrists under his head. "That's it then. Is that what you're saying? We've had this week and that's all?"

She didn't respond immediately, and the room became a box of tension and unsteady breathing.

He stared at the ceiling because the Mae West dressing screen and the popcorn machine, the stage hooks and the marquee headboard all reminded him too much of the life she wanted.

The life that didn't include him.

When she did finally speak, her voice was softly resigned and a little bit sad. "How badly do you want to build your studio in Austin?"

"Badly?" What kind of question was that?

"Would you give that up to be here with me?"

He couldn't answer.

"Exactly," she said, reading his mind. "And what I want means I need to be here. At least for now. Later I might need to be in L.A."

"Austin isn't exactly stuck off in a far corner of the globe." He hated sounding defensive. Making his case. Begging. "I can name you twenty production companies. Hell, Robert Rodriguez's Troublemaker Studios is there."

"So you want me to come with you."

"I didn't say that." If he'd thought for a moment she'd agree, he'd say anything. But he wasn't a big fan of being shot down. "Listen, Shandi. I don't want what we have to be written off because of distance."

This time she at least looked over. He felt her gaze taking him in before she asked, "You don't think your business is still going to require trips to both coasts?"

He shrugged, certain he wasn't going to like where this was going. "I'm hoping no more than once or twice a year."

"So come see me when you're here."

Rolling to his side, he faced her, challenged her. "You said you didn't want to live your life waiting for me to come back to town."

"I won't be waiting," she said without smiling. "I'll be busy."

He was right. He didn't like it at all. "I may not get back for six months."

"I'm not going anywhere. I'll still be around."

"Around and unavailable."

"Are you kidding? I don't have time to sleep much less time to devote to a relationship."

God, she made him want to laugh. How could he hurt this badly and still want to laugh? "Even if the relationship was with me?"

"With you...how can I answer that? I can't even consider it when I know it's not going to happen. It can't happen."

"Because of where we both live."

"It's more than where we live. You know that." She turned her head, only her head, meeting his gaze, her eyes dewy and looking as miserable as he felt. "It's that we both have plans and dreams and things we want to do with our lives."

He knew that. She wasn't telling him anything he hadn't thought about countless times.

She blew out a long, shaky breath, flexed her fingers, then slid them up to twine with his. "I would never ask you to give up your studio to be here with me. And I wouldn't like you very much if you wanted me to give up my dreams."

"Would you like me if I asked you to think about coming with me while we figure a way to make this happen?" he asked, holding her hand as if his whole future depended on her reply. "Not to give me an answer now but just think on it?"

"Oh, Quentin." She caught back a sob. "Don't do this to me."

He leaned over, pulled her close to his body, knowing it was time to let the subject go. "Would you like me better if I held you while you slept?"

"Yes," she said with a shiver. "I'd like that a lot."

11

On Saturday, Shandi didn't manage to roll out of bed until noon. She would've stayed longer, would've slept until it was time for her shift at Erotique.

But she'd agreed to meet Kit in her office at two to do her makeup for the fund-raiser that evening and needed coffee before she'd be able to pry open her eyes.

Otherwise she was likely to make a mess of her friend's face.

It would have been nice to wake up and find Quentin still in bed—Shandi had slept right through his leaving.

Especially since Shandi had changed her tune about she and Quentin being together.

Helping to cement her decision was all the talking they had done during the night.

As crazy as she was about him—though she had known him such a very short time—she didn't want to get used to their sleeping together.

She couldn't afford to get used to their sleeping together.

Having him here with her now, sharing this one

amazing adventurous week, was beyond anything she would ever have imagined.

And she was going to have to convince herself to be content with that. To enjoy this time out of time and expect nothing more.

She was not going to think about his invitation. She couldn't let herself believe that it was real. He didn't really want her—or any woman—to get in the way of his plans. She was different, that was all.

He wasn't used to her independence, her need to make it on her own. Given time and distance, he'd come to realize the idea of having her with him was nothing more than enjoying the ways she stood out in the crowd.

She knew there were women who came to the city hoping to latch on to an industry contact, to win over high-powered men like Quentin Marks, to take them to bed in exchange for their professional connections.

It made it easy to understand his cynicism as well as his interest in her.

If most of the women he ran into wanted something from him or used him for what he could do, why wouldn't he be distrustful?

Fighting that constant sense of skepticism had to be a hard way to live. A sad way to live.

She hated that such a brilliant, beautiful man had been forced to look at the world through glasses colored with suspicion that she doubted were rosy at all.

A big part of her wanted to kiss him and make him all better. To prove to him there were good women out there wanting him for who he was and not for his public image. And if they'd had time, she would.

Oh, hell, who was she kidding. If they had time, she'd fall straight in love. And that was her biggest fear. Her biggest thrill, too. That she'd do just that.

Was doing just that.

Had done just that.

Groaning, she padded her way to the kitchen for caffeine, pushing away the unsettling emotions and remembering instead all the things she loved sharing with him.

Like cuddling up with him. That after-sex nuzzling she loved to do. The talking long into the night after making love.

Not once had he rolled over and fallen asleep. In fact, she was the one likely to drop off if either of them did. She was the one working *and* going to school *and* making time to play with him.

Sure, he had his meetings, and she didn't even want to imagine the stress involved in the decisions he faced—decisions making hers about where to live pale in comparison.

But the man never seemed tired, other than that one night early in the week after a day of meetings. She wanted to tap into his energy source, because he would never have any reason to use it all.

And if his ability to run, run, run was what it took to be successful, she was doomed to failure before she ever got off the ground.

While the coffee beans ground, she glanced across

the main room to see that Evan's door stood open. Either he'd never come home or he was already up and gone.

Even though he existed on less sleep than she did, she'd bet on the former.

He and April seemed even more cozy than usual since they'd made the decision to live together. Neither one had said a thing about whether or not they were sharing April's bed, and Shandi wasn't about to ask.

It wasn't her business, for one thing.

For another, she was having enough trouble of her own having Quentin in her bed.

What in the world was she supposed to do when she was falling in love with a man she couldn't have?

Right now the only thing she could do was shower and dress, pack up her things and get on the road. She had a very long twenty-four hours ahead and then the photo shoot taking up most of tomorrow.

Meaning she needed to gear up now for the nonstop weekend. Coffee poured and laced, she headed to the bathroom to get started doing just that.

Two hours later in Kit's office, Shandi dropped the bag with her work clothes and personal toiletries in one of the two visitor's chairs, her professional makeup case and the bag with her clothes for tonight's midnight date in the other.

Kit was nowhere to be seen and a series of calls to the obvious spots in the hotel turned up nothing. Shandi used the wait to walk down the quiet subbasement hallway and call Quentin's room from a house phone.

Doing her best not to turn into a nag, she hadn't asked him last night what his plans were for today. He was a busy man. She assumed his whole day was scheduled. It surprised her when he picked up the phone.

"What are you doing?" she asked, settling into a plush love seat. "I thought you'd be out wheeling and dealing and making music magic."

"It's Saturday. I'm being a bum."

She grinned to herself, imagining him propped up in bed with a room-service tray and the television remote. "Surely there's some nubile young talent waiting to be discovered."

He growled in her ear. "Speaking of nubile young talent, where are you and why aren't you in my bed?"

Oh, but he made her heart flip-flop. "I'm wandering the halls looking for Kit. She has a fund-raiser tonight and I'm doing her makeup."

"And after that?"

"Depends on the timing. I've got a hot date tonight after work. I might need to rest up before then."

"I've got a bed you can use."

She knew all about what happened in his bed and none of it involved resting. "How about we relax and watch a movie instead? If I remember correctly, we were supposed to do that on our first date."

"You want to go to a movie?"

"Not go to. Watch. As long as the screening room isn't booked for the afternoon." A long shot, but one worth looking into.

"What time?"

Leaning down, Shandi scratched Eartha Kitty's back as the hotel's black cat crept out from beneath the side table, twining in and out of her legs. "I shouldn't be but an hour with Kit. I'll check with the concierge about the schedule for the room, so meet me there at three?"

"If it's booked?"

"We'll cross that bridge...yada yada." She stopped herself from suggesting they order up a movie and watch it in his room. That would mean watching it in his bed.

And that would mean no rest for her weary body. "Just meet me there."

Quentin agreed, though with a lot of grumbling about how comfortable he was, how much more so he'd be with her in his room instead, then clicked off.

Smiling, Shandi hung up the phone, enjoying his pique much more than she should.

She spent another few minutes playing with the cat before returning to Kit's office and was just in time to see the other woman fairly fly out her door and into the hallway, glancing right then left. A band held Kit's hair back from her face that she'd obviously just scrubbed clean.

"There you are." Kit waved her arms excitedly. "I saw your things, but I'm such a mess I don't know if you can help."

"Are you kidding?" Shandi asked, following her girlfriend back inside and closing the door. "Makeup always helps."

"Not this time it won't." Kit scurried about clearing

a space on the side wall's credenza for Shandi to work. "I told you about my escort for tonight, right?"

Opening her multilevel train case, Shandi nodded. "Orlando Bloom's older and way sexier brother."

"Right. That's him," Kit said, finding an electrical outlet for the lighted three-way mirror she took from Shandi's hand. "It seems he's considering Hush for his own thirtieth birthday bash."

"Hmm." Shandi fastened a drape around Kit's neck and shoulders once the other woman had pulled her desk chair up to the credenza. "Can't get anyone to throw him a party so he's throwing one for himself?"

"No. Well, yes. But it's really more about who he'll have on his guest list." Kit heaved a deep breath. "Apparently he has little to do with the family's gallery."

"Except for raising funds."

"Yes. And he's helping to do that by inviting most of his clients to the fund-raiser tonight."

Distracted, Shandi searched through the case for the colors she wanted to use. She chose a moisturizer first. "Who are his clients?"

"He's an agent. In Hollywood. God, I'm so stupid. It never even occurred to me to wonder why the guest list was so weighted with celebrities." Kit closed her eyes while Shandi massaged the lotion into her skin. "I mean, I assumed the family had connections..."

Shandi picked up the trailing sentence. "Just not that you'd be dating the source."

"Yes. Exactly. God that feels so good." She let her

head fall back as Shandi massaged her jawline and chin. "How are you handling it? Dating a star?"

Focused on selecting a base and blush, powder, sponges and her favorite brush, Shandi took a minute to answer. A minute allowing her to gather her thoughts about the truth of her relationship with Quentin.

She wasn't handling it well at all, this dating-a-star business. For one thing, she wasn't sure they *were* dating. For another... "It's one night, Kit. You're a volunteer. He's your escort."

Kit opened one eye and glared at Shandi's reflection. "Thanks for bursting *that* bubble."

"That wasn't what I meant," she said, stepping in front of Kit to apply foundation. "You deal with celebrities all the time. You're great with people. Remember when Dash Black stayed here? The two of you were so comfortable together no one would ever have known you weren't lifelong friends."

The glare this time was two eyed. "You're missing the point, Shandi. I wasn't dating Dash."

"Which I'm sure his woman appreciated," Shandi teased, working to smooth out the soft rosy blush. "Celebrities are people, too—uh, some of them anyway. Dash was. Quentin is. Even Constantine Hale is a regular guy. Go in expecting Orlando's brother to be the same and you'll do fine."

"I hope so," Kit said, closing her eyes at Shandi's direction. "I still can't believe I missed hearing him sing. Constantine. That had to have been amazing."

Amazing wasn't even the half of it. Shandi didn't

think she'd ever get over what his song had made her feel. She knew she'd never forget it. The longing, the ache, the uncommon need connecting two people. The words sung in a voice rumored to melt hearts.

Her mind drifted to Quentin, and she couldn't help but glance at the clock on Kit's wall. Thirty more minutes. An eternity when she had no patience to wait.

Sighing, she turned back to her eyeliners and shadows, choosing a soft taupe-tinted mauve and an outrageously bright gold-flecked pink.

The magic of blending the two colors would take time. The outcome would be stunning. The concentration required would keep her mind in the moment and off the man upstairs. Right now work was her salvation.

She wondered if it would save her later, once Quentin was gone.

MIRACULOUSLY THE SCREENING room was available.

During the week it was booked solid. Usually weekend nights, too, Shandi told Quentin as they shut the door and flipped the switch that would activate the light above it out in the hallway.

Not a guarantee of total privacy, but it would warn others the room was in use.

Quentin would've preferred Shandi in his bed, but this should be fun, too. The last time he'd taken in a show was…who knew?

"What are you in the mood for?" she asked, bending down to look through the DVD library stored in a cabinet at the rear of the room. Film screenings for visiting movie-industry types were run from the sliproom located adjacent. "Horror, comedy, drama, mystery, romance?"

"You decide." He didn't care what they watched. He was only here because being with her was a hell of a better way to spend his time than alone.

"You sure?" she asked, and he glanced over to see her reading the credits on the back of a storage case. "I don't even know what you like."

"Anything." He couldn't remember the last movie he'd paid much attention to. Either his mind drifted to work or he let the white noise of the soundtrack lull him to sleep.

He wandered the room while she made her choice, checking out what he could of the sound system. From what he'd learned of the hotel during his stay, the owners of Hush hadn't scrimped on a thing—the screening room included.

The setup was quality, from the eight-foot-by-four-foot screen to the acoustics to the lighting. The plush crimson-red room and gold deco accents rivaled any he'd seen in the L.A. homes of industry professionals.

"I've got it," Shandi called out, closing up the cabinet after loading her chosen DVD. "You want popcorn or a soda? I can call down to the kitchen."

He shook his head. "I'm saving room for dinner."

Shandi glanced at him, then at her watch. "Dinner's, like, hours away. And that's if we're lucky and Armand doesn't mind covering the last two hours of my shift."

"I'll survive."

"Fine. If I die of starvation between now and then, you have no one but yourself to blame," she grumbled.

Once they'd settled into two of the reclining theater chairs, choosing to sit in the first row in the center, she used a wireless remote to dim the lighting and start the movie.

Only it wasn't a movie.

It was a DVD of Hale's Fallen Angels 2003 world tour.

Quentin glanced over at her where she sat cross-legged in her chair, wide-eyed and riveted by the larger-than-life-size Constantine Hale singing on-screen. "Very funny."

At that she dissolved into laughter. "Hey, you're the one who said to pick anything. Besides, how could I resist after hearing Constantine sing in the bar?"

"Uh-huh," he said and snorted.

"Okay, the truth?" She scooted around, pulling her feet up into the chair and sitting sideways. "It was the name Quentin Marks listed as coproducer that hooked me."

The intense challenge in her gaze should've warned him. He shrugged. "Connie's idea. I didn't do a damn thing."

Shandi narrowed her eyes. "Why do I find that hard to believe?"

"Because of your suspicious nature?"

"What?" she asked, all huffy and frustrated and waving one arm. "Are you going to deny your involvement in a cool project like this because you think I'll be more interested in what you've done professionally than I am in you?"

"No." That wasn't what he was doing. Or if it was, he wasn't conscious of the reason. "The truth is that I really *didn't* do a damn thing. Connie thought my name would help sales of the disc."

"Right." She twisted forward and away in her seat again, as if she thought he was holding back juicy secrets he didn't want her to know. "You just don't like it that I think Constantine Hale is hot."

Well, that much was true, even if admitting to his jealousy wasn't a particularly proud moment. Enlightening, yes. Insightful, ditto.

Because it was also the moment when his feelings for Shandi fell into place.

As unlikely as it seemed, he was tumbling hard and fast. And for the first time in his life, he wasn't scrambling backward to escape.

In fact, he couldn't keep his smile from taking over his heart as well as his face.

He'd been up in his room watching CNN and rehashing the week's meetings when she'd called. Hearing her on the phone had taken his mind off everything, had put a new perspective on the way he wanted to be spending his time.

He wanted to be spending it here—or anywhere— as long as he could spend it with her. He'd never realized that when the right woman came along, she'd be equally important to his days as his work, his future, his continued success.

Equally or even more.

Now he had to figure out how to convince her he was serious when he told her he wanted her with him.

The real challenge, though, was how to make it happen when their goals kept them so far apart.

"You're right," he finally said, gesturing toward the screen as he teased. "He is hot. I like that thing he does letting his hair fall into his face, then looking out from between the strands."

Shandi was silent for several seconds before looking over with a scowl and punching him in the shoulder. "Don't make fun of me."

Rubbing at the spot of contact, he laughed. "Sweetheart, I only make fun because you make it all so easy. Besides, I'm nuts about you."

She continued to scowl, though he swore her mouth trembled. "You're just plain ol' nuts."

He wiggled both brows. "Why don't you come closer and say that?"

"Hmph." She scooted to the far side of her chair. "If I come closer, you're going to get me in trouble for inappropriate workplace behavior."

He held out both hands shoulder high. "I promise to keep my hands to myself."

"Well, I wouldn't want you to go that far," she said after considering his terms, crawling over the wide padded arm into his seat where there was room enough for two.

"That's better," he said as she tucked herself down beside him.

She cast him a sideways glance. "At least from over here I don't have to worry that you're paying more attention to Constantine than to me."

He couldn't help it. He laughed so loud that he forced Shandi to cover her ears. "I promise, my only interest in Connie is his friendship and his career. You can ogle him all you want."

Shaking her head and threatening to punch him again, she turned her attention back to the screen, after several minutes asking, "That song he sang last night in the bar. Is the band going to record it?"

Trade secrets. Insider news. He'd always kept what he knew to himself, not wanting to jinx a project. But this time he felt the urge to get her feedback and input.

"Between you and me?" he asked and waited for her to answer.

She looked over, a strangely guarded look in her eyes. "Of course. As much as I talk? I do know how to keep my mouth shut."

That was good enough for him. "I'm hoping to convince the band to move to my label. Or at least talk Connie into recording his solo effort for me."

"Wow. That would be some coup."

It would be. One that would go a long way to sending his bottom line from red into black. "A way to get my name out there."

"I'm pretty sure your name is already out there."

"In the background, sure. And with the studios where I've produced most of my work." He took a deep breath. "This is different."

"It'll be great," she said, leaning against him as if knowing how much the contact pleased him. How much her approval meant.

"Speaking of plans…" He shifted his upper body, wrapped an arm around her shoulders. "What are you doing with your name to get a buzz going?"

She sighed, deflated, beside him. "Right now nothing. I know, I know. I'm not being aggressive enough. But here's the thing," she added, gesturing with one hand before he could interrupt. "I have to support myself, which means I can't do an internship until I'm finished with school. I don't have time and I'm allergic to living in cardboard boxes."

The tangents she took tickled him every time. "Cardboard boxes?"

She nodded fiercely. "If I don't work extra shifts once I move in with Evan and April, that's where I'll be living. In a box. Down by the river."

"So what's up with the moving thing?"

"It's going to happen, I guess." She shrugged. "Unless the kids get married."

The kids. Funny. Uh, *wait a minute*. "Married? What're you talking about?"

"It's complicated," she hedged, looking back toward the screen.

He reached for the wireless remote she'd left in the seat of her chair and lowered Connie's volume. "I've got nothing but time."

"The reason I'm the one living with Evan is because his grandmother doesn't believe unwed couples have any business cohabiting. Since my relationship with him is platonic, I pass muster. Though barely."

"So they're going to get married in order to have her approval to live there?" He might be a cynical bastard but he knew that didn't make sense.

"That's what I asked April."

"And?"

"She said if they got married it would be because they wanted to spend the rest of their lives together. Because they were in love."

"The freebie living arrangements have nothing to do with it?" he asked.

Shandi shook her head, wisps of blond hair flying. She pushed them back. "April says the marriage is inevitable. Why give up the good apartment if moving up the date helps them keep it?"

"I'm surprised she wouldn't be holding out for a big, fancy wedding." He supposed he was being judgmental, but hey. "She seems the type."

"She is the type. Which is why hearing her say it didn't matter pretty much floored me. Especially because it's not just the fancy wedding."

"How so?"

"She'll be giving up a cushy lifestyle to be with Evan. I'm shocked that she has it in her. But really proud, you know?" Quentin heard Shandi's smile in her voice. "She's been doing a lot of growing up lately. That can't be a bad thing. Even if I end up on the street."

"I won't let you end up on the street."

"Yeah, yeah." She waved one hand. "So you keep saying."

He glanced down. "What about you?"

"What about me?" she asked, scowling.

"Are you the big, fancy wedding type?"

"Are you kidding?" She snorted. "I doubt I'm even the marrying type."

"Married to your career and all that?"

This time she was the one to look up and over. "Isn't that what you've done?"

He shrugged, not exactly comfortable with where she'd taken the conversation. "I think of her more as a mistress than a wife."

"Oh, I see. All the fun without being dragged down by the baggage?"

"No. It's just that until now it wouldn't have been fair to foist my lifestyle on a woman." It wouldn't have been too fair to himself either. Missing the intimacy that came with the commitment.

"What about the future? Once you get set up in your studio?" Her voice softened, dropped to a whisper. "Do you think you'll get married?"

"I don't know. I'm pretty set in my ways. I don't know if anyone will have me." *Or if I'll find anyone I want,* he kept himself from saying.

He couldn't say it when he knew that, given the chance, he was ready to see where he could take things with Shandi. All he needed was a hint from her that she was willing to take the same leap.

"Give yourself a few months in Austin to shed your

cynicism." She reached down, patted his knee. "I bet you'll be surprised at what you see once you're looking forward instead of running away."

"Are you always this damn deep?"

"I'm a bartender. It comes with the job."

12

Shandi—Pay the tab you signed the other night or have it deducted from your check. Let payroll know by Monday morning. Oh, I'm taking you up on that offer and taking off Tuesday night. If you think you'll need help, have HR call in a temp.
Armand

"YOU KNOW, IF I'M NOT careful with these hours I'm keeping I'm going to lose my job *and* flunk out of school when I've only got two semesters to go. If that happens, I won't be able to afford the rent on even a cardboard box. Then where will I be—broke and uneducated and homeless and unemployed?"

Not that Shandi cared. Okay, she cared. And she *had* worked until midnight, only taking off the last two hours of her shift.

The crowd in Erotique had been smaller than usual for a Saturday night. Not surprising at all since a new piece of sensual performance art was premiering in Exhibit A, and the show came complete with complimentary champagne and Chef's famous hors d'oeuvres.

Shandi had also left a message on payroll's voice

mail before clocking out. Now to wring the tab money out of Evan to cover the deduction in her check. Or else he could buy all of next week's groceries.

Armand had given her his blessing to leave since, after seeing his note posted on the board in the bar's back room, she'd agreed to cover him Tuesday, her usual night off. And it *was* the weekend, so she didn't have class tomorrow.

There. The analysis made her feel a bit better.

Still, having Quentin take her out on the town was worth whatever she had to pay, because the night they'd just spent out was one no man she'd ever dated would have thought to put together, much less been able to afford or organize without pulling a lot of strings.

She wanted to hate that Quentin had pulled strings, but she couldn't. It had been a dream date—the man, the dinner, the dancing. The carriage ride. All of it into the wee hours of Sunday morning. He'd made special arrangements. Used his clout, promised favors.

And he'd done it for her, to be with her.

She hooked her arm through his as they walked back to the hotel, her feet aching in her heels when she was used to the practical leather lace-ups she wore when tending bar. She didn't care about that either.

All she cared about was keeping the fantasy night from ending. Unfortunately it was doing that way too soon.

"Where you would be," Quentin said, getting back to her rhetorical question, "is in a better place to take me up on my offer and come with me to Austin."

Sigh and double sigh. She didn't want to get into this

tonight. She wanted tonight to be pure girlie-girl, castle-in-the-sky, Cinderella time. Dealing with real life could wait for the sun. "You mean your offer that makes no sense since I still won't have my degree or money to live on?"

He glanced over and down. "I have money. And trust me, with the studio contacts I can make? You won't need your degree."

"Quentin Marks." She jerked her arm from his, lurched to a stop and thrust her hands to her hips. "What in the world is wrong with you?"

"What?" He turned toward her where she'd stopped a half block from the hotel's entrance. "I'm not allowed to call in markers on behalf of a friend?"

"No," she said, wondering why, after her haranguing of the past week, he still didn't get it. "Because then I'd be indebted to you, and I'm really trying to do this career thing on my own."

He mirrored her stance, hung his head. "Can we forget about this career thing for tonight?

"I don't know, can we?" She crossed her arms, knowing she needed to drop it or risk ruining what of the fantasy night remained. "It seems like it's taken on a life of it's own."

"My fault. I wasn't thinking." At her glare, he came closer and acquiesced. "I know. I'm sorry. It's just hard for me to get my head around the fact that I'm going to have to give you up."

"I know." She rubbed her hands up and down her arms, shivering as she absorbed his words.

"I don't think you do, Shandi. You're the best thing that's ever happened to me." He looked toward the street, looked back after finding his words. "And with all the pull I have professionally, I can't do a damn thing to find a way for us to be together."

"We're together now," she offered softly, certain that very soon her heart was going to break. How could what had been a night of unbelievable delight quickly turn so glum?

He stared at her, the wind whipping strands of his hair that had escaped from his leather band, his eyes filled with confusion and longing. "Are you coming in with me or am I taking you home?"

"That depends."

"On?"

Oh, but it was going to hurt to say what she had to say when he was standing so close and she wanted so much to step into his arms. "On whether or not you can let everything go and enjoy what we have left."

"You mean the whole forty-eight hours?" he asked, his tone impatient.

She gathered the blowing ends of her wrap tighter, wondering whether the ache in her chest was disappointment or anger or love. "I think I'll just grab a taxi."

"No." He reached out, took hold of her hand. "I don't want to fight, Shandi. Not unless it means we can kiss and make up."

She felt the warmth of his fingers, the intent in his hold. He wanted her, needed her. And wasn't that all she was asking for? She squeezed back before moving into his embrace. "I suppose we can stay here. I hear the rooms are nice."

He heaved a huge sigh of relief. "The rooms are beyond nice."

"I don't think I ever got to see all of yours."

"I'll be glad to give you a personal tour."

"Okay," she said, taking a breath to settle her nerves and her hands that wouldn't stop shaking as they crossed the lobby and headed for the elevators. It didn't work as well as she'd hoped.

Star Wars couldn't hold a candle to her raging internal battle.

Should she stay the course or take Quentin up on his offer for a free ride?

What kind of choice was that? In the end, his contacts would be invaluable. No one made it in this industry without connections. It was a given of the lifestyle she'd chosen as her own. She knew all that.

But for two years now she'd stood her ground. She'd worked her ass off temping until landing the Erotique job. She spent five mornings a week in class. She scrimped and scratched and clawed to make ends meet.

So why was the idea of letting the man she was coming to love provide for her, help her realize her dream, giving her such holy hell?

Wasn't that what a relationship was based on? Give and take and support that came in every color—emotional, mental, financial, spiritual?

She could buy all of that if this were truly a relationship. And that was the rub. The fact that it wasn't. It was a fling. A fabulous fling, yes.

But Quentin would be gone in another forty-eight hours. And nowhere in his invitation to come along had he mentioned his feelings for her.

Okay, he'd said he didn't want to give up what they had without exploring where they might take it.

That was close enough, wasn't it? After all, she hadn't admitted her growing feelings to him.

Did that mean it was simply her pride in the way? That she was so determined to prove her family wrong that she was jeopardizing her own best chance for success?

Dear Lord, she was so confused.

The elevator door opened onto the sixteenth floor and, as they had their first night together, they made their way to his room. Only this time they weren't laughing and adjusting their clothing as they hurried down the hallway.

This time they walked silently side by side. This time they had a history. What happened between them tonight wouldn't be about discovering each other and reveling in the excitement of that first time.

Tonight would be about appreciating the treasures they'd uncovered. About wondering where they were going to go once the night came to an end.

Even knowing she would spend the day with him— along with her friends, working on her project—didn't ease the sadness and loss weighing her down.

She leaned against the wall next to the door and let Quentin walk past her into the room. He turned back when he realized she hadn't followed, questioning her with no more than a hint of a smile.

She sighed, kicked off her shoes and made her way toward him, leaning into his chest. It took him no time to respond. He held her close, rocked her side to side.

"Are you okay?" he whispered.

She felt the warmth of his breath, smelled the brandy-laced coffee they'd shared before returning to the hotel. "I'll be fine. Just allow me a melancholy moment."

"Not sure I want to do that." He stroked her back and she shivered. "Melancholy isn't the mood I was hoping for here."

She cuddled closer, enjoyed it when he tightened his hold. "What mood were you going for? Uh, besides the obvious?"

"I was going to bring you the moon and the stars."

"Really?" She stepped back, looked up into his eyes. "How so?"

He arched a brow, the room's low light casting his face into shadows. "You'll be okay here for a minute? You won't fall apart on me or anything?"

She nodded. "I'm fine."

He nodded, too. And then, holding her by the shoulders, he dropped a kiss on her forehead before leaving her to cross the room to the French doors that opened onto his balcony.

They'd been so lucky to have a beautifully flawless sky all night; she'd told him during the carriage ride how much she wished they could stay out until morning.

He hadn't been quite as captivated, his interest being less on the blanket of indigo above and more on the one he'd told her covered his king-size bed.

She watched now as he pulled the plush covering of deep reds and purples, blues and golds from the bed and spread it on the floor. He added the throw pillows, as well as the decorative bolsters that gave the room the decadent feel of a sultan's palace.

Playing the part of his harem girl was not going to take any acting skills at all—even if he was the one setting the stage for seduction, sliding the suite's low coffee table closer to the door and opening the lid of the carved and gilt-edged box that sat on top.

Inside were vials of scented oil, one of the room's many sensual amenities—as opposed to the more overtly sexual ones in the matching box he brought over from the glass-fronted armoire. She knew the box was locked, just as she knew what she would see inside once it was opened.

If it was opened.

He leaned down, placed the key on top, then stood slowly, capturing her gaze, telling her without words that he was giving her that power, leaving the decision on whether or not to unlock it, to use and enjoy what was inside, up to her.

And so before he had a chance to say anything, she dropped her wrap, walked across the room to where he was waiting and did just that. Turned the key on the toy box and opened the lid.

She didn't look inside. Neither did Quentin.

But his eyes flared, and his chest begin to rise and fall rapidly. And it didn't surprise her a bit when he swore under his breath, seeking control, and headed back to the room's wet bar for two tumblers and the brandy decanter.

He poured himself a drink, continuing to mutter to himself, then tossed it back. He swallowed, hissed, waited for the burn to subside.

"Better now?" she asked.

"No." He returned to the armoire and turned on the stereo system already set to play some mood-setting sexy jazz tracks. "I wish I knew what the hell it is that you do to me so I could stop it."

Her fingers went to the row of buttons beneath the deep-cut neck of her sleeveless black dress. "Is that what you want to do? Stop it?"

Speechless, he shook his head and stared. The more buttons she released, the more skin she revealed, until she reached the last one at her bikini line.

She started to shrug off the garment.

He stopped her, reached for her, peeled the rayon down her arms, baring her breasts, her belly, her mesh thong.

This time his hiss was long and low, his heated gaze devouring.

"I'll take that as a no?" she asked, stepping out of the pool of her dress onto the sultan's bed, the moonlight shining into the dark room and onto the bright strands woven into the blanket's fabric.

"A big fat one," he said, his hands going to work on

his own shirt buttons, his shoes, his socks, the fly of his trousers, until he stood before her in nothing but his wonderfully revealing boxer briefs.

"So I see," she said with a prurient grin she couldn't help. And then she held out her hands. He took them in his, stepped onto the blanket and slowly lowered them both to their knees.

Once there, facing each other, bodies pressed close, he kissed her, cupping her face with one hand, her nape with the other, sliding his fingers into the fall of her hair and winding the strands around his wrist.

He moved his lips from her mouth to her chin, her neck, tasting her throat, licking and nibbling his way from the hollow of her throat to her breasts. He sucked one breast, and she groaned as the sensation spiraled through her body.

She tightened her sex and held the feeling close, moving her hands from his shoulders to his waist, where she encountered the elastic band of his boxers and the tip of his erection straining to be free.

She didn't wait, didn't ask. She wanted to touch him and so she did, easing the fabric over the bulge of his cock's ripe head and down the length of his shaft that was thick and veined and pulsing with the flow of his blood.

While he got out of his shorts, she turned to the box on the table, her heart pounding at the thought of sharing with Quentin the pleasure found inside. She chose a soft leather cock ring and asked his permission with only the lift of one brow.

He gave a single nod. She supposed that was about all he could manage what with the way his pulse was popping in the vein at his temple. She wrapped the strap around the base of his shaft, enclosing his sac, her eyes on his as she tightened the weighted leather ties.

He shuddered at the constriction and the pull, closed his eyes as she fondled his balls, as she wet her fingers with the sticky moisture he'd already released and used it to ease her way farther between his legs.

He spread his knees wider, giving her the access she wanted. She played with the ridged extension of his erection, with the puckered flesh behind, returning to slide a finger between his balls, separating his sac and rolling his jewels in the cup of her palm.

His eyes were still closed, his jaw taut, his hands laced together on top of his head. And so she leaned forward, ran the tip of her tongue around one nipple, then the other, before dipping down and taking his cock into her mouth.

She worked her tongue along the seam beneath the sensitive head, sucked the plump mushroom cap between her lips. Holding him with one hand, she explored between his legs with the other, gauging his release by his pulse and the constriction of the sac around his balls.

It didn't take him long. His hands came down to grip her shoulders, and his hips began to thrust. She continued the pressure and suction of her lips, releasing the leather strap she'd bound around him.

He came in bursts of warmth, which she caught with

the cup of her tongue, and she stayed with him until he was finished, giving him the pleasure of her love in the most intimate way she knew how to do.

She waited until his shudders had finished before she released him, tossing the cock ring to the wastebasket near the armoire as he collapsed into the throne of pillows piled on the blanket.

He looked up at her from where he lay on his back. "Give me five. That's all I need."

Men were just too cute, she thought as she stretched out beside him. "Take as long as you need. I'm not going anywhere. And just so you know, my favorite scents are herbal and citrus."

"Three more minutes, and you're in for the massage of your life," he said, his breathing beginning the long return to normal.

Turning onto her belly, she raised up onto her elbows, tucking a pillow beneath her, and stared out the open doors at the wide expanse of the sky. "I wonder what sort of view I'll have should I end up having to move."

He turned his head toward her. "When will you know if you're going to have to?"

She shrugged, shook her head. "After the photo shoot tomorrow I plan to corral either April or Evan—or both if I can—and get some sort of concrete answer. If I know what's going on, I can deal. It's the uncertainty and the waiting that's making me nuts."

Quentin rolled onto his side, rested his palm in the small of her back, rubbing circles there for several seconds before saying, "You know I'll help you any way I can."

His hesitation endeared him to her even more. She knew what it cost him to hold back, to offer what to him was no doubt so little.

He could've offered—again—to set her up in her own place, to pay her way through school, to call in all those markers on her behalf.

But he hadn't. He simply lay at her side, caressing her and letting her know he was there for her, that he wouldn't let her starve or end up in a cardboard box.

She glanced over, her eyes watering, and leaned close to kiss the tip of his nose, laughing as she pulled away.

Instead of laughing with her, he frowned. "What was that for?"

"For being you. For paying attention." She was enjoying his warmth at her side and the night air blowing over her skin.

"Ah. Herbs and citrus, right?" he asked, getting to his knees and crawling across her body to study the bottles of massage oil in the gilt-edged box.

"That, yes. But you also managed to bite that generous tongue of yours."

"Generous, huh?" he asked, settling in behind her, his knees straddling her legs. "I guess I'll take that as a compliment."

"It's meant as one. And I thank you for the reassuring offer." Knowing she had somewhere to turn should worse come to worse made the future easier to face.

"Promise me you'll come to me before you hit your cardboard-box bottom," he said, rubbing his palms together to warm the oil he'd chosen that smelled like a mixture of basil and nectarine.

"Mmm. I promise." She closed her eyes, wiggled and shivered beneath him, feeling his soft penis stir against her bottom when she did. "That smells so good."

"I hope it feels good," he said, starting at her shoulders, kneading the muscles there and making his way down to her biceps before returning to the base of her skull.

"Unbelievable," was all she could say. She felt as if she were drifting toward unconsciousness on one of those cotton-ball Oklahoma clouds. "See, this is why we'd never work together. I'd want this treatment all the time, and you'd get tired of pampering me."

"Who says I would?" he asked, his thumbs working the muscles along either side of her spine, his weight settled on her hips holding her still. "I'm enjoying this probably more than you are."

"Oh, that's not possible," she argued, even as she felt his erection stiffen between the cheeks of her backside and smiled to herself.

He moved lower then, pressing the heels of his palms into the upper curves of her bottom, manipulating her flesh and muscles until she moaned.

"See?" she muttered. "Not possible."

His responding laugh was low and husky and as raw as the words he mumbled, as carnal as the motion of his lower body as he stroked his cock over her, settling the weight of his balls against the lower curves of her ass.

She lifted her hips, dislodging him and pulling her

knees up beneath her so that the height of her backside fit perfectly against his groin. He moved in behind her then, pushed two pillows beneath her stomach before reaching for the bottle of scented oil.

He poured a small circle onto the cleft of her bottom; the oil pooled and ran between her legs, lubricating her for his questing fingers that followed. He teased the seam where her thighs met her hips with his index fingers, used his thumbs to spread open her cheeks.

She trembled there on the sultan's bed, surrounded by pillows and moonlight and Quentin's warmth. She loved his touch, his thorough tenderness as he aroused her, seeking out her response.

She couldn't get enough of that thing he did with his knuckle...*yes, that.* Right there. Pushing up against her entrance, teasing her and pulling away to circle her clit, rubbing along either side.

It was all she could do not to cry out. But she wanted to wait, to let him play and discover her body's secrets.

The wait wasn't easy, not with his cock as well as his fingers between her legs. He held himself and guided the tight head between her folds, teasing her entrance without slipping inside where she wanted him desperately.

She wiggled, pushed back, leaning onto one elbow and using her free hand to coax him to give her what she wanted. She failed on all counts. He pulled away, chuckling as he continued to tease her.

And then he got serious. He sat behind her, spread his legs on either side of hers and leaned in to replace his fingers with his tongue, pushing inside of her while his hands held her open.

She gasped, groaned, shivered and reached down to press the side of her clit. The stimulation only caused another burst of sensation that brought her that much closer to the orgasm she wanted to save.

And then she gave up. She couldn't help it. Quentin pushed two fingers inside of her and stroked her, licking at her and whispering words that urged her to come.

The burst of sensation consumed her. She shuddered and trembled and shook. Her belly burned. Her nipples scraped the blanket as she squirmed. It was an orgasmic flash fire, and over way too soon—

Except Quentin had other plans. He urged her to turn onto her back, to draw her knees to her chest, to open her legs as he crawled above her, as he braced himself on his knees and pushed the head of his cock into her sex.

He didn't move except to fill her, to lower his hips until his body lay flush against hers. And then he propped his elbows on either side of her head, brushed her hair back from her face and stared into her eyes as he begin to move.

It was like nothing she'd ever experienced, this intimacy, this incredible connection of both bodies and souls. Her heart pounded fiercely. She ached from her chest to her belly.

Oh, God, but she loved this man.

She loved his kindness. She loved how he was never selfish, how he always thought of her, looked out for her, tended to her—whether they were in bed, walking in a garden rooftop, sharing a meal of spinach-and-chicken roll-ups or watching a concert DVD.

She loved his determination, his drive, the way he'd made himself into the man he was. She loved the man he was. And when he wiped away the tears running from her eyes to her temples, she shook her head and smiled.

And then she wrapped her arms around his neck and held him close while she loved him, while they moved together as if they had both finally come home.

13

EVEN THOUGH IT HAD BEEN close to four o'clock by the time she'd finally arrived home, Shandi was up by nine Sunday morning.

Today was the only day she would have to make this photo shoot work. Evan was off. Kit was off. April was always off. And Quentin wasn't yet due to leave town. They'd all agreed to meet in the hotel basement at Exhibit A at ten.

Tomorrow everything changed. Work schedules and school schedules and travel schedules would muck things up. This was her one and only shot at getting this right.

If it didn't work, she'd have to arrange a new time with Kit and April and give up the idea of Quentin as her marketing trump card.

It was bad enough she was going to have to give him up as her lover. After last night she didn't know how she was going to do it, tell him goodbye, let him go.

She told herself to make the most of these last two or three days. She didn't know if she'd see him on Tuesday before he flew out.

But she would see him today, all day, and for that she was grateful. She wasn't going to spend the time moping about what was to come.

She was going to enjoy him, and if she found a way to let him know of her feelings, she would. Not in any sort of twisted effort to convince him to stay with her or make him regret having to leave.

Simply so that he would know what an amazing memory he'd always be. How much she had enjoyed having him in her life. And how very very much she wished things could have been different between them.

But things were what they were, so she packed up her stuff and headed for the hotel. The subway was delayed, and she arrived to find April and Evan already there, sitting cuddled up on one of the bar's banquettes.

Rolling her eyes, Shandi glanced around, realizing how much different the place looked without the billowing smoke with the trace of mint scent or the blue lights casting a seductive—if not eerie—glow over the white room.

Walking farther inside, she saw that her friends weren't just cuddled up but were drinking coffee and sharing a plate of Chef's famous Bouche s'mores made with house marshmallows and imported chocolate.

No doubt Kit's handiwork—though the other woman was nowhere to be seen. Neither was Quentin. Obviously April and Evan had spent yet another cozy night at April's place and needed the jump-start of sugar and caffeine.

Hmm. On second thought, that didn't sound so bad.

Shandi had to clear her throat twice before they looked up. "Are you two going to scarf down all of that yourself or could you possibly share?"

April looked up, smiling. "Hey, Shan. Scoot on in here. Kit went to get more coffee and another plate. Oh my God, I've never eaten anything this good in my life."

"What, the Carters of Connecticut don't melt marshmallows over campfires?" She bit into one of the squares and realized she'd never eaten anything this good in her life. "Uh, never mind. I think Chef has cornered the market."

"No joke," Evan added. "And I don't even like chocolate that much."

The door opened again and Shandi looked up to see Kit usher Quentin inside, another plate of s'mores in her hand while he carried one of the kitchen's thermal carafes and a small crate of mugs, sugar and cream.

Shandi didn't say a word. She just watched, breathless, thinking of their last hours together, her body heating in response, her heart warming with joy.

He set everything in the center of the large circular table that during showtimes would be covered with a cloth, then leaned down to kiss a smudge of chocolate from the corner of her mouth before grabbing a s'more of his own.

Her friends giggled, and Shandi wanted to roll her eyes. But she couldn't. Quentin had captured her gaze and she couldn't move.

He was the most beautiful man she'd ever known,

and she ached with the power of just how much she loved him.

Kit slid onto the banquette to chat with April and Evan and pour coffee for everyone else, leaving Shandi with nothing to do but stare as Quentin finished off a marshmallow-and-chocolate concoction, then reached for his cup.

"Did you get any sleep last night?" he asked, lifting the fresh brew and blowing across the steaming surface. "You look tired."

"A few hours," she admitted, noting that he, of course, looked as if he'd just slept for weeks. "I'm pretty much running on adrenaline."

"You'll get some rest once we're done here?" It was a simple question, asked with the nonchalance of a casual friend.

But she heard everything he didn't say bubbling beneath the surface in a cauldron of emotionally charged words.

They were the same ones she wanted to use to tell him how what they'd done last night had changed her world. To tell him that she loved him. That she wondered what she was going to do once he left her, left the city, left a huge gaping hole in her life.

Instead she shrugged and reached for the caffeine. "If I have time. My shift starts at six."

"Then we should get started, yes?" He arched a brow, signaling that she needed to take care of herself, that he intended to see that she did.

Breathless, she nodded, glancing at the other three

in the photo-shoot party. "Evan, I thought we'd use the platform and see how that goes. Quentin can help you. So if you want to get started setting up your equipment, I'll work with the girls on their makeup and hair."

"Sure thing," Evan said, washing down the rest of his breakfast with his coffee and waiting for Kit to slide out of the booth so he could follow.

Shandi got to her feet, as well. So did April. Both women had done nothing more than wash and blow-dry their hair as straight as possible.

Shandi glanced from one fresh face to the other. "You brought your clothes, right?"

Kit nodded, gestured to the banquette on the other side of the one in which they'd been sitting. "Hanging behind us. Shoes and everything."

After working out her concept days ago, Shandi had raided the closets of both April and Kit looking for outfits in the color scheme she'd chosen.

Not surprisingly, considering the size of the two wardrobes, she'd come up with exactly what she'd hoped to find, right down to the shoes.

"And you?" she asked, looking back at Quentin now that she could breathe again.

He held his arms out to the sides. "What you see is what you get."

What she saw worked. In a very big way. He was wearing the unstructured ivory linen suit he'd had on that night she'd sat on his lap in the library...a memory that she quickly forced away.

She would have preferred a color that was a shade

or two darker, that of bamboo or coconut skin, a blend of Kit's chocolate brown sheath and April's silk tank shift that was just this side of white.

But she hadn't been about to ask him to buy a new suit for an ad that was a simple class project that she hoped turned out as brilliantly as she'd envisioned.

"You'll do," she said, ignoring the spark in his eyes and gesturing with an index finger. "Though you'll need to lose the band. This is about hair color. So I need to be able to see your hair."

One brow cocked, he reached back, pulled loose the strip of leather and shook his hair free. The strands fell like a cascade of caramel, and Shandi swore she heard the other two women behind her sigh.

She loved his wildly mussed look, hated his wildly mussed look, wished they were back in his room so she could muss him up even more. He was perfect for the king-of-the-jungle slant of her ad.

Suddenly she just wasn't sure she wanted to share her own private Quentin with her girlfriends or the women in her class. Not when the two beside her were in need of a shovel to pick up their dropped jaws.

The next hour in the basement room was spent in prep. The girls were able to use the electrical outlets, for Shandi's mirrors and straightening irons, in the booth that controlled the bar's sound system, lighting and smoke machine.

She managed to deflect the questions about her relationship with Quentin with the standard reply that he was a temporary diversion and would be gone from her life in two days. It didn't work. Her girlfriends were relentless.

While Shandi chose a foundation, April was the first to start in. "Seriously, Shan. I know how important all this makeup-artist-as-a-career thing is to you—"

"A career *thing?*" Shandi glared at April's reflection in the mirror. "What's that supposed to mean?"

"You know." April leaned forward to check the shadows beneath her eyes. "A career thing. And please tell me you have concealer."

One of Shandi's brows went up. "Like your gallery and jewelry design is a career thing? Or like Kit's PR work is a career thing?"

"Sure. Why not? It's just that the point comes where you have to ask yourself—where we all have to ask ourselves—what we're willing to sacrifice. The man for the career or the career for the man."

What? Now April was channeling Dr. Phil? Shandi started in with her sponge, smoothing the sheer color. "So those are the only two choices?"

"You have others?"

"Yes, I have others. What about sacrificing dreams and goals and self-respect and one's identity and—"

"Okay, okay." Kit held up both hands, laughing. "I think wc get the point."

"You may," April said. "I certainly don't."

"I can't believe you," Shandi said, jamming her hands to her hips. "You're the one letting your family stand in the way of your love life."

"You're right. I have been." April turned in her chair

and looked up to meet Shandi's gaze. "But I've also been thinking a lot lately about that choice."

She felt a prickle of unease at that. She turned back to her case for brushes and blush. "And have you come up with any brilliant conclusions?"

"I don't know about brilliant," April said, studying her nails. "But I do know that I haven't been fair to Evan or to myself."

Wow. That certainly shut Shandi up. She went to work on April's cheekbones. "Does that mean you're going to cut your ties with your family or finally introduce him to your parents?"

"I'm actually considering a combination. And," April went on, pointing a finger at Shandi, "I owe it all to you."

Shandi's hands stilled. "To me? How so?"

"Because of who you are. You make no bones about your priorities. You've done what you've had to do to get what you want, including stepping on your family's toes on your way out the door."

"If it had only been toes, it would've been a lot easier," Shandi admitted, surprised to learn that her own personal battle had influenced April. "It was more like I crushed everything they believe about family, as if I counted it no more important than a vat of grapes I would stomp into wine."

"Wow," Kit said. "That's deep."

"No. It's sad. And constricting. And demoralizing. Can you imagine your own family telling you what to do with your life? And telling you doing anything else means you have no respect for them?"

Both April and Kit fell silent. Shandi, too. She hadn't meant to blow up like that, she mused, rummaging for eye-shadow colors that ran the gamut from cream to terra-cotta to sienna to rich chocolate-brown. She'd accepted her family's narrow outlook for what it was.

Their inability to deal with change. Their prejudice against progress. Their refusal to embrace what they didn't understand or anything that fell outside of their comfort zone.

But their way of seeing the world meant that she'd had to make the choice to leave that safety net behind or be strangled by it. And she wasn't sure she still wasn't trailing pieces of the webbing with her.

Because here she was still basing what she did on how they would react when doing so tied her to them as much as if she still lived in their white-frame house on the outskirts of Round-Up.

"But enough about my life," she finally said with a bittersweet laugh. "Let's get you two beauties on stage. And while you're there keep your paws off my man."

The next half hour was spent applying and blending colors to eyes, lips and cheeks, as well as taming the two contrasting heads of hair. The three women giggled about good dates and bad dates and all manner of in-betweens while Shandi tended to the others, perfecting their look.

"So all that heavy-duty rhetoric about career and family doesn't change a thing, does it?" Once Shandi began packing away the tools of her trade, Kit stood, smoothed down the slimming lines of her sheath, her blond hair giving off a near-white sheen. "It's still all about the birds and the bees and that crazy little thing called love."

"Don't look at me if you're going to be using the *L* word," Shandi scoffed, turning off her lighted mirrors and the straightening irons. "I've got a project due in two weeks, no time to be standing here swooning."

"Right," April said, dusting a brush over the shine on her nose one last time. "You're the one who made the chocolate mess when your *man* came into the room."

"Yeah, yeah," Shandi groused, herding the two back into Exhibit A's main room. Now was not the time to continue this conversation.

Evan had set up his lighting equipment around the circular platform and positioned his tripod off to the side. For now, his camera hung around his neck. And as Shandi had instructed, he'd set two of the funky black chairs borrowed from Erotique on the stage.

As much as she owed Quentin for helping her out, she owed Kit just as much for clearing the personal use of the room with Janice. They had a window of four hours before the crew would arrive to begin setting up the bar for tonight. Which meant the show needed to get on the road.

But as Evan helped situate both women in the chairs on the stage, Shandi had eyes only for Quentin. She'd deferred to her photographer's expertise and hadn't touched a hair on his head. While Kit and April both defined the word *sleek,* Quentin was the antithesis.

He was, in fact, the epitome of wild. From the glint in his eyes that reminded her so clearly of what they'd done last night to the way his hair appeared to have been styled by a lover while she writhed beneath him.

He looked like sex. Living, breathing sex. And as much as she tried to focus on Evan's directions, she finally had to back away to the closest banquette and sit. Sit and watch and try not to drool.

Okay, it wasn't that bad. But it was very, very close. She did her best to remain analytical, critical, an artist at work. When that failed totally, she worked to assume the role of impartial bystander, a spectator enjoying a show.

Nothing. It wasn't happening. All she could think about was getting her hands on him, kissing him, tearing him out of his clothes. That and the way he made her laugh and hope. The way he teased her and took all that she dished out.

He was a good man and he cared about her future, her happiness. About her.

And seeing him now up on that stage, straddling the bar chair in reverse, his arms braced along the top, his feet hooked on the stabilizing rungs, the fit of his clothing revealing the body beneath…

Oh, but she was in such serious trouble here.

Kit stood on his right, her back to him, her arms crossed over her chest, her feet spread wide. April stood on his left in a mirror position. They were the lionesses of his pride. The blonde and the brunette. The colors of their shoes and clothing the reverse of their own. Quentin was the king. The protector, the leader, the virile and savage beast.

And Shandi thought she would die from the way she wanted to belong to him, to be his mate for life.

ONCE AGAIN, EVAN COULDN'T sleep, the cause of his insomnia nothing new. For the past year since they'd started dating, he'd been spending half his nights on April's sofa, sleeping only a fraction of the hours he was there.

Now that he was spending his nights in her bed, he wasn't sleeping at all.

Neither was he having sex.

Celibacy hadn't been a problem when he'd slept out in the other room. And it wasn't so much a problem in here either. Except that it was.

He respected that she wanted to wait and that their waiting would continue until they were married. But being this close to her was a physical burden he thought he'd be better equipped to bear.

When she'd told him she wanted him near, he knew sleeping beside her wasn't going to be the cakewalk he'd convinced himself he could make it. Taking matters into his own hands only cooled him temporarily.

And that wasn't the least bit hard to understand. Hell, he could grow hard standing behind the coffee bar at work simply by looking up and catching April's eye should she smile at him over the rim of her cup.

He loved her. He wanted to make love with her.

Instead he moved away and turned onto his side, hugging the far edge of the bed and counting wolves. With the night he was having, he wasn't surprised when he closed his eyes to find they'd eaten the sheep.

Less than thirty seconds later April asked, "You're not sleeping, are you?"

"Not for a lack of trying."

"Can we talk?"

"Sure." He started to roll to his back but waited. It just seemed smart to let her set the course, to make the first move. He didn't want to embark on one that was wrong.

"This hasn't been fair, me asking you to sleep in here with me," she said, taking a deep breath. "I know you haven't complained, but I also know that neither one of us is sleeping worth a damn."

He smiled to himself. April so seldom cursed it was strange to hear even the tamest of swear words come out of her mouth. "I can move back to the couch. Or I can just stay at the apartment. Whatever you think is best."

"What I think is best is that we stop waiting."

Time froze. He froze. The air froze, her words crackling like icicles waiting to fall. "Waiting? For sex?"

"Yes." Another deep breath. Another exhalation. "And no."

He wasn't sure which was the good news and which was the bad. "If you have a solution, I'm listening."

"I do, but I don't want you to think less of me for suggesting it." The covers rustled as she moved.

Okay. This time he was rolling over. He'd keep his hands to himself, the sheet tucked down between them. But he needed to see her face.

Her face was beautiful. Soft in the light filtering in through the tiny slit above the blinds in the window. She'd hooked her hair behind her ear, and a tiny diamond stud—she'd told him the earrings were an eighteenth birthday gift from her parents—sparkled on her lobe.

"April, talk to me. I could never think less of you for anything you think or say."

"Well, you should. I'm a horrible person at times." Tears glistened in the corners of her eyes. "Selfish and material, and I don't pay the attention to you and your feelings that a fiancée should."

His heart thudded. "Is that what you are now? My fiancée?"

She nodded. "I'd like to be."

He reached over, ran an index finger around the shell of her ear. "How long of an engagement were you planning?"

"That depends. Are you particular about the type of wedding we have?"

He chuckled. "Hardly. I'm the pauper in this relationship, remember? I seriously doubt my grandmother would unlock that tight wad of hers for much of anything."

"Especially since you're marrying me."

What could he say? "She is who she is. Generous

when it suits her needs. Penny-pinching when it doesn't. And trust me, me getting married doesn't suit at all."

April sighed, rolled onto her back, pulled the comforter up beneath her chin. "Does it suit you?"

She asked the question so softly, he wasn't sure that he was hearing what she was trying to say. "Yes. Of course. Why would you ask me that?"

"Because if it suits you," she said, turning only her head to make eye contact, "and if you're not set on a big fancy wedding, then I'd like to make a suggestion."

He didn't think it was possible to care less about a wedding. "Does it involve anything illegal, immoral, wicked or depraved?"

"No." Smiling, she shook her head on the pillow. "Unless you have a problem cutting classes for two days."

14

"I'VE DONE SOMETHING YOU'RE probably going to hate me for," Quentin said as, still rubbing the sleep from her eyes, Shandi pulled open her door at what felt like the crack of dawn Monday morning.

"Uh, okay." She tugged her ratty chenille bathrobe tighter, wishing he had called before coming so she'd at least have brushed her teeth.

He walked by her into the room without waiting for her invitation. "Tomorrow's your night off, right?"

"Usually." And Tuesday usually was. She shut the door, locked it again. "I'm working for Armand."

"You were. You're not now." Hands at his hips, Quentin studied the floor a long moment before looking back up. "This is that thing you're going to hate."

"Hate?" Right. He'd said something about that earlier. Ugh, she wasn't even awake enough to process anything; why was he here? "What did you do?"

"I threw around my Grammy-winning-record-producer reputation and got you two nights off in a row," he said, his guilty expression out of proportion to his crime.

Two nights off in a row didn't sound so bad. At least, not right now when she was as tired as she was. "Why?"

"Because I'm taking you to Austin with me."

She frowned, muzzy-headed and things taking way too long to clear. "I thought you were leaving tomorrow."

"I was. I changed my mind." He was so animated she couldn't look away. His smile bright. His eyes brighter. "I'm ready to get home, but I want to take you with me."

Argh! How many times did they have to go through this? "I don't want to go to Texas," she whined.

He held up both hands. "It's not to stay. It's just a visit. I want you to see my place and the lot where I'm going to build my studio."

She backed up, unsteady, stumbled her way to the table and sat. Quentin moved into the kitchen, rummaged through her cabinets for a mug, found the coffee beans already in the grinder and hit the switch.

She sat at the table and watched him make himself at home. He filled her coffeemaker with filtered water, measured out the freshly ground beans, hovered while the carafe filled as if wanting to be sure she got the hottest and freshest cup possible.

How could she adore him one minute and be so frustrated with him the next? He was kind and thoughtful, one of that breed of a few good men. He wanted to take care of her, to help her reach her goals.

He'd offered her an alternative to the several years of struggling that lay ahead. Was she insane to let her pride stand in the way? Was she trying to prove to him that she wasn't like the women who wanted to use him?

Or was she trying to prove to herself that she could do anything she set her mind to and make it on her own? To prove to her family that they were wrong about her? That she wasn't going to fail as they'd predicted?

She supposed it was a mixture of all of the above. What she feared most, however, was that taking Quentin up on his offer would mean that she had failed. That her family had been right about her all along.

That she was nothing but a long-legged, willowy cat's tail of a filly who served drinks in the Thirsty Rattler, as did all the Fosseys of Round-Up. But she was more. She had to be more. She knew she was, as did Quentin.

And that was the bottom line, wasn't it? What she thought about herself even more than what he thought about her? She loved him and was certain he was falling in love with her. He showed his feelings in everything he did.

Sighing, she rested her head on the table and watched him—an activity that was easy to do. She'd spent so much time doing it yesterday at the photo shoot that she'd had trouble focusing on the bigger picture of the project.

She groaned at the thought. "I'm so going to flunk out of school."

"What? Just because you couldn't keep your eyes off my ass, you think your project's going to bomb?"

She lifted her head just enough to stick out her tongue. "Evan's supposed to burn the pictures to a CD today. I guess I'll see later whether I need to start shopping for a cardboard box."

"No, because later you'll be in Texas."

"Oh, right. Remind me why I'm going?"

He didn't answer immediately. He didn't even look over when she asked.

All he did was pour her a cup of coffee and carry it to the table along with a spoon, the two pink packets of sweetener he knew that she'd use and a half-pint carton of cream from the fridge.

Only then did he finally take time to reply. "I'm not ready to write you out of my life. The other night, Saturday—or Sunday morning, I guess it was—when we made love... And we did make love, Shandi. That wasn't just sex."

"I know," she admitted, because he wasn't going to go on until she'd given him a response.

"It was singular and beautiful and it's what makes a relationship work." He paused, swallowed. "That sort of bond. That connection. It's intimate and raw and totally pure. And so very rare."

Then his gaze dropped to his hands on the table. "I'm not going to lie and say I've never taken advantage of the sexual favors that have come my way. What I will say is that I gave up casual sex a long time ago because of what those encounters taught me."

"What *did* they teach you?" she asked, feeling suddenly cold and wrapping her hands around her mug to steal away what she could of its warmth.

"That the best sex is had between the ears." A tender smile crossed his face, and he looked back up. "Corny, but there you have it. I can scratch a physical itch myself. There's no awkward after-sex hassle, and I don't have to give myself instructions."

She sputtered coffee, almost choked. "Don't do that. I'm not awake enough to swallow and laugh at the same time."

"I promise. Never again" he said, grinning. "Just know that I like not having to give instructions. I like the way you've intuitively picked up on what makes me tick. Like I said—rare. Very rare."

He shoved her coffee cup closer. "So drink up and get dressed and pack whatever you'll need for the next two days. I want you to meet the real Quentin Marks."

SHANDI STARED SILENTLY out the window as they began their descent into Austin. She remembered this sky. Oklahoma might be four hundred miles away, but the sky was the same. Big and bright and endless.

She hadn't been back even once since leaving home fifteen months ago. Her work schedule was always nuts over the holidays. And it was easier to stay in the city and keep busy than to go back to Round-Up and face the constant haranguing over the choices she was making in her life.

But being here now with Quentin, transferring from the jet once it landed to the limo for the long ride out to his place, she didn't feel any of the anxiety or disquiet she'd expected.

Instead she felt as if she was exactly where she belonged.

It was the same feeling she'd experienced Sunday morning when they'd made love.

And that scared her half to death.

As if sensing the drain on her emotions, he shifted in the cushy leather seat and urged her closer, wrapping an arm around her shoulders and dropping a kiss on her forehead. He didn't say a word. He just held her.

She couldn't have asked for a more perfect response. And, of course, it was a response that made her want to cry.

Instead she placed her hand on the inside of his thigh, tucking her fingers close to his knee. "Does it ever wear off? The thrill of hiring private jets and limos to get around?"

"The thrill?" He gave a small, noncommittal shrug. "I suppose it has. What hasn't is appreciating the convenience and the privacy."

She closed her eyes, leaned back her head. "I suppose that would make the cost worth it."

"I don't think about the cost. I'm traveling for business, so it's a write-off."

"Right. I forgot." She hated how he could say one thing and make her feel like a rube. Her own insecurities. She knew him well enough to know he wasn't strutting his stuff. "I'm hanging with a big-league player."

"No, sweetheart." He lifted a hand, stroked a finger along her jaw. "You're hanging with a man who would pay double the price if it would get him home any faster."

That one thing told her so much about him, reinforcing what she already knew but doing so in a way that she hadn't been able to appreciate until now.

She was ready to see him in his element. To meet the true Quentin Marks. To learn everything she could about the man at her side in order to make the decisions she needed to make.

The biggest one being whether or not to tell him that she'd fallen in love.

"IT'S TRUE. YOU'RE THE first woman I've brought home since building this house."

He'd given her the full tour of the four-bedroom, two-story, cedar-and-glass house earlier, and now Shandi sat at the marble bar of brick-red separating the dining area of the tiled great room from the kitchen where Quentin sliced onions and peppers. Out on the patio, chicken fajitas were on the grill.

"It's not that I don't believe you," she said. "I just don't get it."

"Why not?" he asked, concentrating on the vegetables so that he didn't get caught up in looking at Shandi in his kitchen and end up chopping off his thumb. "I'm not here enough to entertain. Or at least, I haven't been."

"No. I mean, I just don't get why you haven't dated when you're at home." She reached up, twisted her hair, tossed it behind her shoulders. "Or do you only indulge in all that extracurricular activity when you're traveling? A woman in every port and all that."

"I don't visit ports. And I don't have women anywhere. The only one I have is in my kitchen." She was itching for an argument, and he didn't know why. "And she happens to be the only one I want anywhere."

She grinned, but he felt the distance. "You don't have to sweet-talk me to get me into your bed, Quentin. The fajitas will do it."

"I swear," he grumbled, smacking the flat of the knife blade against the cutting board and glancing over. "I can't decide if you're the most frustrating woman I've ever known or just the only one whose grief is worth putting up with."

"Grief? You think I give you grief?" At that, she laughed. "You haven't been around many grief-givers in your life. You ought to take a hop and a skip up to Oklahoma and meet the Fosseys of Round-Up if you want to know grief."

This was it, wasn't it? Being in Texas. Being too close to Oklahoma and the past from which she'd run away. He laid down the knife, washed his hands and dried them, then turned to face her, his hands at his waist. "Let's go."

"What?" she asked, her frown tinged with panic, her voice the same.

"We've got time," he said after glancing at his watch. "It'll take most of the night to make the drive, but why not? We can stay over, and I can show you my studio plans when we get back tomorrow."

"Uh, no thanks. I'd rather not." She climbed down from the bar stool, never looking at him as she made her way out through the sliding glass doors to the cedar deck, where smoke from the charcoal fire swirled in the summer wind.

Quentin shook his head and sighed, staring out the kitchen window and watching as she hugged herself tightly, ignoring the covered hot tub in one corner, the umbrella table in the other, choosing to stand at the railing and lose herself in thought.

He knew it instinctively. This thing with her family was what he needed to get her to talk about. That was her hang-up. More than her career and his career and the clashing of their two outlooks on pursuing success, whatever had happened when she'd left Oklahoma was what was driving—or killing her—now.

Leaving the vegetables and the knife on the cutting board, he grabbed two Corona longnecks from the fridge and went out to join her. She didn't even glance at him until he forced her to by handing her the beer. "Tell me about it."

"About what?" she asked, twisting the top from the bottle.

"About Oklahoma. Not about the Thirsty Rattler or your parents or your brother and his wife. Tell me about leaving. About why you can't go back."

"It doesn't matter." She lifted the bottle, drank, set it on the railing and still didn't meet his gaze. "And I can go back. I just haven't. I just don't."

"There's got to be a reason," he prodded as he opened his own beer.

"I'm busy. I work. I go to school. I'm broke. Take your pick." Finally she glanced over briefly. Her eyes had lost their sparkle. "It's going to be a while before I'm used to private jets and limos and staying in hotels like Hush."

"I know that," he said, because it was benign enough for these waters he was treading carefully.

She snorted then. "Hell, the time it's taking me to get my degree, I'll be too old to enjoy a hotel like Hush once I can afford it. That ought to make the Fosseys of Round-Up very happy."

He waited, uncertain how far to push or if he should just let it go. But he couldn't. They wouldn't get anywhere until they got past this. "Your family doesn't believe in you, do they? They predicted that you'd fail."

"Oh, no. It's more clichéd than that." She drank deeply from her bottle before rushing out with the rest. "They're waiting for me to run home with my tail tucked between my legs. It's been over a year, and you can bet they're still looking out the window every time they hear a car in the driveway."

So that was the reason she wouldn't take his help. Making it on her own was more about proving herself to her family than anything. "They'll be waiting forever, Shandi. You and I both know that."

"Then you know more than I do," she said bitterly.

He backed up, leaned against the deck's umbrella table, giving Shandi space. "I do know. I believe in you completely."

When she didn't respond, he took a deep breath, an equally deep pull on his beer and continued. "Because of that faith, here's what I'd like to do. And please hear me out before knocking me down flat."

She turned to face him, leaned into the corner of the railing. "What?" she asked, biting off the word.

"I know you want to finish your degree. That's— what?—two more semesters?" She nodded. He went on. "And I know you don't have the money or collateral you need to go into business for yourself."

"Keep going. I'm waiting for you to tell me something I don't know."

"Okay then. What you don't know is that I believe in you so much that I'm willing to finance you." He watched her stiffen, hurried on. "I talked to my finance guy before we left the city—"

"About me? You talked to people about me?"

He nodded. "About your goals. About your drive and determination. About your talent. About backing you."

"You want to buy me?" she asked, her voice breaking. "So that I'll stay here with you?"

"No, Shandi. I want to help you. I have the money and the connections. I want to offer you what I have, as a loan—call it whatever—to get you started."

"A bribe?"

He ignored the barb. He knew she was hurting. "If you want, sure. You can continue your education, but you can also be building your professional résumé."

She waited several seconds before she replied. "So this wouldn't be here."

"It would be wherever you wanted it to be.

Here—" he caught himself before adding *with me* "—or in New York or L.A. if that's what you want."

"Why would you do that?" she asked, tears leaking from the corners of her eyes.

Oh, boy, he thought, his heart pumping like a piston. Was this the simplest question she'd asked of him today. "Because I love you."

SHANDI RETURNED TO THE deck long after she and Quentin had made sweet love in his bed. She'd pulled on the shirt he'd been wearing and left him there. She couldn't sleep and didn't want to wake him.

She would be returning to New York tomorrow, in less than eighteen hours, on the same private jet in which they'd arrived this afternoon. The brevity of her stay meant they had little time to do more than eat, sleep, tour the house and go over his studio plans.

Quick trip down, quick trip back. No time for sightseeing or seeing his friends. As much as she would have liked to have met them, she had to say she really didn't mind.

After his offer to take her to Oklahoma, she wasn't in a social mood. And after his declaration of love, she was lost as to what to say or do next.

Dear Lord, was she ever at a loss.

They'd eaten fajitas on the deck and watched the sun go down. A beautiful summer night, breezy and warm, just this side of hot. They'd talked of inconsequential things while enjoying the solitude and the view.

For the first time while in his company she'd found

herself tongue-tied with little to say. In fact, she hadn't been able to think. She'd barely been able to breathe.

She hadn't tasted a thing she'd eaten and had spent the evening with her heart in her throat, hearing the echo of his declaration of love. Hearing her responding silence.

Why hadn't she told him that she loved him, too?

The rest of the night had been passed the same way. Conversation swathed in long silences while watching the stars twinkle overhead in the amazing expanse of sky.

She was so conflicted. His love in one hand, her life in the other. It made what she'd thought a simple decision impossible to make.

She should have been able to tell him no thank you and return to the life she'd sworn to everyone around her that she loved. And she did. Truly.

Quentin's loving her shouldn't change anything any more than did her love for him.

Funny thing about love. It changed everything.

15

ANNOUNCEMENT
Whoever took the extra blue bulbs from
Exhibit A's control room,
You have 24 HOURS to put them back!
ANNOUNCEMENT

"WHAT IS GOING ON WITH YOU two?" Shandi asked when April and Evan climbed up to sit at the end of the bar—Quentin's end of the bar—on Wednesday night. Evan looking like the cat. April looking like the canary.

Shandi was highly suspicious.

She hadn't seen either of them since they'd wrapped up the photo shoot Sunday afternoon. She didn't even know if they realized she'd been gone from Monday noon until Tuesday night.

If they did, they obviously didn't think much of it since they hadn't said a word.

Instead April stared at Shandi as if she was the one who needed to be doing the questioning. So Shandi set Evan's beer and April's Cosmopolitan on the bar and did. "Okay. I give up. What's going on here?"

"Aren't you even going to ask us where we've been

since Monday?" April asked, reaching for her drink and cuddling up into Evan's right side. He leaned over and kissed the top of her head.

Shandi tried not to roll her eyes; the lovebirds were going to make her sick. "Actually, I didn't know you'd been anywhere."

April gasped, nearly spilling her drink as she set it back on the bar. "How could you not know? We haven't been at school or at the apartment."

Shandi hedged, reaching beneath the bar for her water and uncapping the bottle. "Uh, neither have I."

"Where have *you* been?" Evan asked before sucking down a quarter of his beer.

"In Texas."

At that he sputtered. "What the hell were you doing in Texas? Oh, wait. I know."

He looked at April, who answered for him as if he didn't have a brain. "She went with Quentin."

Their voices in unison, they asked, "Well?"

Good freaking grief. Had they finally had sex or were they just attached so completely they were now sharing the same vocal *and* umbilical cords? "Yes. I went with Quentin."

"And?" April moved forward, her eyes wide. "What happened?"

"Nothing really," Shandi admitted, taking a drink of her water, then adding, "I came back. He stayed there." What more was there to say?

Evan sat back in his seat. "So what's next? Are you going back? Is he staying there?"

Hello? Was she talking to herself? Shandi crossed her arms and glared. "What is this? The Spanish Inquisition?"

"No. Just the Harcourt Inquisition."

It wasn't the way April giggled when Evan said it as much as the overall feeling that something weird was going on with them that gave Shandi the final clue.

She looked from one to the other, smiling and shaking her head. "The Harcourt Inquisition. You went to Vegas, didn't you? You two goons got married."

April nodded. "We decided to do it Sunday night, and flew out first thing Monday morning."

"When did you get back?"

"Today," Evan said. "And we've just come from visiting with my grandmother."

Shandi felt her eyes widen. "Do I need to sit down?"

"Only if you tend to pass out from good news."

"She's letting you keep the apartment." Shandi stated the obvious with a huge sigh of relief.

"No. She's letting *us* keep the apartment," Evan reminded her. "The only person who's going to be moving is April. We're headed to her place now to start packing up extras to send into storage. Then we'll go through my stuff and do the same. It'll be a squeeze, but we'll get it all in."

"Have you told your parents yet?" Shandi asked.

Shaking her head, April looked over at her new husband. "We're going down to Connecticut tomorrow. Either they disown me or they don't. It doesn't matter. I'm with the man I love, and that's all that matters."

It was wonderful news. The news Shandi had been hoping for. At least, the news about the apartment. No extra shifts. No second job. So why wasn't she feeling the love?

Because instead she was feeling like the third wheel on their cozy bicycle built for two.

"This is great. Seriously." She glanced up in time to see Constantine Hale cross through the lobby, and then all she could think about was how much she missed Quentin already. And it had only been one day. "I'm so happy for y'all. Shocked and almost speechless but happy."

Evan shifted forward again, huddled over the bar to get close. "You don't seem so. Or else you don't seem happy for yourself."

"It's weird." Shandi reached for dry cocktail napkins to replace the ones now damp with condensation. And then she glanced from one friend to the other. "I know this is what we've all wanted. The apartment part of it anyway."

"Yes," Evan said. "We have."

"I know, I know. But what I don't know is how I'm going to handle coming home from work to a house that's not empty. I'm too used to you sneaking back in after curfew."

"Well, that's just silly," April said with a mother-hen frown. "I would think you'd feel better knowing we're all there for each other."

"I do, it's just going to be strange. It won't be the same. I won't have two roommates. I'll be living with a married couple." And she wouldn't have the one thing she most wanted—Quentin there with her sharing her own loving bed.

"I don't think it'll be that hard to get used to." Blowing off her worries, Evan reached for his beer. "Hell, it's going to be an adjustment for all of us."

"I suppose." But sitting in front of the window looking at the sky and hearing the sounds of squeaking bedsprings coming from the other end of the apartment? Uh-uh. That wasn't going to work. But she'd deal with it later.

Right now she was feeling an urge to clock out and make the next flight to Texas.

An urge that seemed to have come out of nowhere but that she knew had been close to the surface since yesterday when she'd told Quentin goodbye.

"Anyhow," she said, saving the rest of her thoughts for later. "Tell me about the wedding, but feel free to leave out the details of the wedding night."

"Oh, oh." April waved both hands. "It was the cutest little chapel. Evan tried to talk me into being married by Elvis, but that wasn't going to happen. I was willing to give up the Belgian lace, four-foot train and the eight attendants but not the roses or the doves."

"One dove." Evan held up one finger, twisted his mouth wryly. "In a cage."

Shandi laughed. "Sounds perfect."

"Oh, it was. Except that you weren't there to be our witness," April added with a bit of a pout.

"So let me see your ring," Shandi said, drying her

hands after wiping down the bar. "Did your man here spring for a big chunky rock?"

Fingers spread, April placed her left hand on the bar. "No. He commissioned it."

"From who?"

"Me," April said softly, her voice almost reverent, as was her expression as she looked into Evan's eyes.

"You designed your own wedding band? Oh, April." Shandi picked up April's fingers for a closer look at the wide band of hammered gold and amethyst chips. "It's gorgeous. And so sickeningly romantic."

Tears misted her eyes as she lifted her gaze. "I'm so happy for you two."

And she was. She truly was. But now it was time to get happy for herself.

Suddenly she was certain of what she needed to do to make that happen.

She only hoped she could pull it off.

FLYING OUT OF LA GUARDIA for the second time in a week should've been one of the hardest things Shandi had ever done. In a way it was. She was leaving behind so much. Her job, her classes, her friends.

Telling herself it was temporary, that she'd be back, that the compromise she was making was not a betrayal of all she'd worked toward the last year was easy.

Believing it was harder. Until she reminded herself that her gains would quickly wipe any lingering thoughts of losses from her mind.

She was going to be with Quentin, going to make her life with the man she loved, the man who was her life.

Two semesters remained in her degree plan. She would take the hiatus, certain he would never insist she sacrifice her dream completely. In fact, she knew he wouldn't.

He would do all he could to make it happen for her, including letting her return to school when she was ready. In the meantime, she wouldn't stop him from calling in markers, from making contacts, using his connections.

But she wouldn't take any money unless he agreed the money would be a loan. That was the bottom line of her pride.

The flight seemed to take forever since this time she was suffering none of the negative trepidation she'd suffered before.

Instead her stomach was a bundle of butterfly nerves, swooping and swarming and splashing through the coffee that was the only thing she'd had time for this morning before her taxi arrived.

At long last the plane began its descent into Austin. She stared out the window, seeing nothing of what she'd seen earlier in the week, this time seeing what she thought Quentin must see upon landing.

His home. His future. His life as he wanted to live it. The life she wanted to share.

She only thought once about turning around and taking the next flight back to New York. Only once. Because then she couldn't wait to see him and surprise him and tell him all the things she was feeling.

How much she'd missed seeing him today—the only time she hadn't seen him in the last ten or so days—and how strangely lonely she'd been.

How she'd gone to class and thought of him instead of paying attention as she manipulated her hair-color ad in Photoshop, staring into his eyes there on the screen until she couldn't take it anymore.

She wanted to tell him about rushing home to change for work and finding the flower he'd tucked behind her ear that night during the carriage ride. About wearing it on the subway to Hush and losing it in the crowd.

She wanted to share her feelings over April and Evan's joyful and surprising announcement and over seeing Constantine Hale walk through the lobby and feeling profoundly the absence of her love.

That more than anything was what she wanted him to know. How very much she loved him. How very much she did.

QUENTIN WANDERED FROM HIS kitchen out onto the back deck, from where he stared off into the distance at the setting sun sparkling over Lake Travis.

The view was the reason he'd bought the property and built here. He'd decided way back when that it was the perfect place to sit and enjoy life to the fullest.

A few days ago he'd actually thought he might be enjoying that life with Shandi. She had fit in so perfectly, as corny as it sounded, showing him what it would be like if his house was truly a home.

She'd only spent one night here, yet he'd turned expecting to find her coming toward him so many times since he'd lost count. He did it again now, swearing he heard her footsteps, smelled her scent, heard the crystal bell of her laugh.

He was losing his mind, because there was nothing behind him but his big empty house. He shook his head, leaned into his palms where he'd braced them on the deck's cedar railing and wondered if she'd answer the phone if he called.

Or if she'd see the Austin area code on caller ID and let her machine pick up.

If she'd screen him out, waiting a day to return his call, the next time waiting two days, three the one after that, easing him down slowly since he was obviously too dumb to take the hint.

She didn't want to hurt him by coming out and telling him she'd made her choice. That she'd chosen her career over anything she might feel for him.

That proving herself to her family meant more to her than the fact that she'd already proven herself to him.

He was feeling way too sorry for himself. This was turning out to be a hell of a bad way to start his new life. He needed to suck it up, get on with his plans.

To stop thinking he was smelling her scent, hearing her voice—

"Quentin?"

He turned, his heart pounding. He wasn't imagining anything, because there she was, walking across the flagstone floor of his great room, waving one hand and saying, "Uh, you probably need to turn off your alarm. I sorta broke in and I'm sure it's dialing 911 as we speak."

Crazy wench. He hurried through the sliding glass door, punched the security code into the keypad, barely able to remember the numbers for all the questions running through his head.

He finally asked the only one that mattered. "What are you doing here?"

She moved from the dining area into the kitchen, keeping the bar between them as a buffer. "I came to take you up on your offer."

It wasn't what he wanted to hear, but it was a start. An opening. A door that she hadn't closed. "Good. Okay." She was here for business. But she was here. "I'll call and set up a meeting. We can get started laying out plans tomorrow."

But when he looked over again, he found she stood there with her arms crossed, shaking her head. "No, Quentin. Not that offer."

He laced his hands on top of his head to hold himself in place, afraid he'd reach for her, afraid that wasn't what she wanted. "Which one then, Shandi? Which offer?"

He didn't think he'd seen her expression any more serious than it was when she said, "The one about giving this relationship a fighting chance."

That he could deal with. That was better. They were almost there. "As a long-distance one?"

When she shook her head, he couldn't even move.

All he could do was grin. A big, fat, stupid clown of a grin. "Did you bring your things?"

"I didn't have time to bring anything but me," she said, and he wanted to tell her she'd brought the only thing that mattered.

But then she went on. "I left Evan and April a note to pack me up. I figured it could be on your dime."

"Absolutely. I'll wire them money tomorrow." He'd wire them hundreds of thousands if it meant Shandi would have no reason to go back to New York.

"They went to Vegas and got married."

"Whoa." He wondered how she felt about that, about losing two roommates, about leaving her friends. Wondered even more how she felt about her future being here with him. "Did you want to do that?"

"Which part? Go to Vegas? Or get married?"

"Either. Both. Anything."

She laughed. "Vegas would be a fun trip to take. I've never been."

"Then we'll go."

"Sure," she said, adding, "But when we get married, I was thinking of doing it in Round-Up."

He could only nod.

"And I was thinking of waiting at least a little while. Making sure this really is more than a fling. That it's truly as pure and rare as you told me."

"I don't have any doubt," he barely managed to croak out before he lost the rest of his voice.

She only waited a moment before tearfully whispering, "I don't either."

He opened his arms then, and she stepped into his embrace. And they stood there holding one another, not speaking, not moving, doing nothing more than enjoying the existence of this magic they'd made.

They did it all with the sun outside setting over the lake while the sky twinkled with the stars just waking up.

And in that moment Quentin realized exactly what Shandi saw when she sat and stared at the sky.

She saw possibilities and promises and potential. She was right. About so many things. But about this most of all.

That what they had found together didn't need to be rushed. They would have it forever.

And that the sky truly was the limit.

* * * * *

In October 2005
look for PRIVATE RELATIONS
by Nancy Warren, the
next book in the
Do Not Disturb *miniseries.*

Blaze

HARLEQUIN® Blaze™

Where were you when
the lights went out?

Shane Walker was seducing his best friend in:

#194 NIGHT MOVES
by Julie Kenner July 2005

Adam and Mallory were rekindling
the flames of first love in:

#200 WHY NOT TONIGHT?
by Jacquie D'Alessandro August 2005

Simon Thackery was professing his love...
to his best friend's fiancée in:

#206 DARING IN THE DARK
by Jennifer LaBrecque September 2005

24 Hours:
BLACKOUT

THE SECRET DIARY

A new drama unfolds for six of the state's wealthiest bachelors.

This newest installment continues with

STRICTLY CONFIDENTIAL ATTRACTION

by Brenda Jackson

(Silhouette Desire #1677)

How can you keep a secret when you're living in close quarters? Alison Lind vowed never to reveal her feelings for her boss, Mark Hartman. But that was before she started filling in as nanny to his niece and sleeping just down the hall....

*Available September 2005
at your favorite retail outlet.*

If you enjoyed what you just read,
then we've got an offer you can't resist!

Take 2 bestselling love stories FREE!

Plus get a FREE surprise gift!

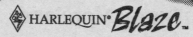

HARLEQUIN® *Blaze*™

Women can upgrade their airline seats,
wardrobes and jobs. If only we could
upgrade our men....

The Man-Handlers
Women who know how to get the best from their men

Join author Karen Kendall as she shows us
how three smart women make over their men
until they get newer, sexier versions!

Catch these irresistible men in

#195 WHO'S ON TOP?
August 2005

#201 UNZIPPED?
September 2005

#207 OPEN INVITATION?
October 2005

Don't miss these fun, sexy stories from Karen Kendall!
Look for these books at your favorite retail outlet.

HARLEQUIN®

Blaze™

COMING NEXT MONTH

#201 UNZIPPED? Karen Kendall
The Man-Handlers, Bk. 2
What happens when a beautiful image consultant meets a stereotypical computer guy? Explosive sex, of course. Shannon Shane is stunned how quickly she falls for her client, Hal Underwood. As the hottie inside emerges, she just can't keep her hands to herself.

#202 SO MANY MEN... Dorie Graham
Sexual Healing, Bk. 2
Sex with Tess McClellan is the best experience Mason Davies has had. Apparently all of her old lovers think so, too, because they're everywhere. Mason would leave, except that he's addicted. He'll just have to convince her she'll always be satisfied with him!

#203 SEX & SENSIBILITY Shannon Hollis
After sensitive Tessa Nichols has a vision of a missing girl, she and former cop Griffin Knox—who falsely arrested her two years ago—work to find her. Ultimately, Tessa has to share with him every spicy, red-hot vision she has, and soon separating fantasy from reality beomes a job perk neither of them anticipated....

#204 HER BODY OF WORK Marie Donovan
Undercover DEA agent Marco Flores was used to expecting the unexpected. But he never dreamed he'd end up on the run—and posing as a model. A nude model! He'd taken the job to protect his brother, but he soon discovered there were undeniable perks. Like having his sculptress, sexy Rey Martinson, wind up as uncovered as he was...

#205 SIMPLY SEX Dawn Atkins
Who knew that guys using matchmakers were so hot? Kylie Falls didn't until she met Cole Sullivan. Too bad she's only his stand-in date. But the sparks between them beg to be explored in a sizzling, delicious fling. And they both know this is temporary...right?

#206 DARING IN THE DARK Jennifer LaBrecque
24 Hours: Blackout, Bk. 3
Simon Thackeray almost has it all—good looks, a good job and good friends. The only thing he's missing is the one woman he wants more than his next breath—the woman who, unfortunately, is engaged to his best friend. It looks hopeless—until a secret confession and a twenty-four-hour blackout give him the chance to prove he's the better man....

HBCNM0805